KISSING BOOTH

RIVER LAURENT

A big, big thank you to...
Leanore Elliott & Brittany Urbaniak

ISBN: 978-1-911608-11-0

✿ Created with Vellum

CHAPTER 1

Dani

"I need your help," Helen explodes into my ear, as soon as I answer my phone.

Oh, Jesus. It's another one of her emergencies. They come like clockwork. At least twice a week somebody calls out for the day and she flies into a panic and calls *me*. If I survive the stress of night school and working for her agency, I'll be thankful for every last damn hair on my head. I stayed up all last night studying because I thought I had today off and could sleep in. Of course, I should know better by now.

"What time is it?" I groan.

It must be really early, because she doesn't answer my question. "Lisa fell and sprained her ankle last night," she frets instead.

"You don't say!" I mutter, turning from my side to my back,

and knocking over the pile of books I'd left lying beside me in bed. Of course, Lisa and her accidents! This time, it's an ankle sprain. A couple of weeks ago, it was a sprained wrist. Before that, a bruised tailbone. A pinched nerve. Always things no one can follow up on since she can't be expected to prove that any of it is true. The bruised tailbone is my favorite, supposedly the result of slipping down the stairs onto her ass. God, I really hope that one, at least, was true.

"You don't need to sound so sarcastic." Helen tuts. "Some people can't help it. They're just accident prone."

I wish I could say, stop with the bullshit, but I know what she's doing. She's making excuses because she doesn't want to lose Lisa, since Lisa handles some of her best clients. I squint at my alarm clock. "I'm sorry, Helen, I really am, but don't you think this is getting a little ridiculous? This was supposed to be my first day off in two weeks, and I'm seriously behind in my Psych homework. I was up studying until four this morning. And according to my clock, it's only freaking six-thirty now."

Helen chuckles, apparently unconcerned by the extent of my sleep deprivation. "If it were anybody else handing me that line, I'd say they were lying."

"But you believe Lisa's lying ass every time," I mutter.

"You, on the other hand," she continues, like she didn't just hear my quip. "Are the one person I can believe is pushing herself that hard. I don't know how you do it."

"Yeah, well, a lot of coffee." I sit up. I need a brain reboot, which always involves a pot of coffee.

"Just for this, and because you're such a terrific sport and somebody I can always count on, I'm giving you Lisa's most prized account. I mean, you're gonna love this. It pays a fortune."

My ears perk up. Well, that's different! "Just how much is a fortune?"

"A thousand dollars," she announces smugly.

My eyes nearly pop out of my head. Whoa? That kind of money for one day of work? "Do I have to give someone a blowjob after I finish cleaning?"

"I know you're joking, so I'll let that go." Her voice is dry. "It's a 4,600 square-foot penthouse. Belongs to some crusty old billionaire, but I'll doubt you'll even see him. Lisa never has."

"You want me to clean a 4600 square foot penthouse in a day?"

"It's in tip-top condition. Hardly any scrubbing. Lisa normally finishes it all in a day. I think he just likes having someone come out to give it the royal treatment before he gets back from his business trips. His secretary said that he won't be back for another two days, but Lisa is booked solid for the rest of the week, so I had to schedule his place today." She pauses while her words sink in. "Any of the other girls would have bitten my hand off for this job, but it's yours, if you want it."

"Yes, I'll take it," I snap, launching myself out of bed, and switching on the coffee maker. The royal treatment simply means a deep clean. I can do a tip-top apartment that size in seven maybe eight hours. A thousand smackers for nine hours work tops. Holy crap. Where do I sign?

"That's wonderful news," she gushes, like she didn't know I

would accept even if it had only paid the usual rates. I'm such a sucker, and she knows it. "Now, there are specifics we'll have to go through first."

I pause in the middle of pouring my coffee into my mug. I knew it was too good to be true. "Specifics?"

"Specifics. He's a very specific type of person. Dani, he's paying a thousand bucks. I think we can give in to a few demands."

I breathe in the fragrant aroma coming from my coffee mug. "Demands. First it was specifics, now it's demands. Should I start getting nervous?"

"If you don't think you can handle them..."

Sometimes I hate Helen. She's more manipulative than a doe-eyed two-year old. I look down at the chipped Formica counter, heavy with unpaid bills. "No, I can handle them," I say, before pouring a half-mug of coffee down my throat. Something tells me I'm going to need it today.

"Great," she coos happily.

"Where is it, by the way?"

"Central Park West."

"Naturally." If he could afford to pay that much for a cleaning service...

"Do you have a pen handy?"

Jeez. How long is this list of specifics and demands? I scramble back to bed and grab my pen. I open my notebook. "Right. Shoot."

"First, you have to wear shoe covers the moment you walk inside. He doesn't like the carpets getting dirty."

"I thought that was why people took their shoes off before entering a home."

"He doesn't want that. No socks or tights, nothing like that on his floors."

"Wow! He sounds like a party animal." I write it down. "Where would I even get them?"

"I don't know. Walmart, probably. If Lisa can find them…"

"Right, right. Next?"

"A hair net, too."

"Am I cleaning his bathroom, or cooking his food?"

She snorts. "We'll get to the bathrooms in a minute."

I exhale. *Suck it up, Dani. It's not every day you get to make a thousand for a day's work.*

"You can't use bleach. Fresh lemon or orange juice, white vinegar and baking soda only."

I scribble it down. "Hmm…that's interesting. Do you know why?"

"He hates the smell and it's unhealthy," she explained.

"Is he a germaphobe?"

"No. Just very particular, and very health-conscious."

"Okay. That, I can get behind." Even if my treadmill makes a better clothes hanger than it does a means of exercise.

By the time we finish, I've filled out two pages. Both sides. "This is a lot, Helen. And Lisa does this on her own?"

"She does, though she'll sometimes split the job between two days when there's a decent amount of time before the client gets back to town. Though, we don't have two days. You're booked tomorrow at Mrs. Sheldon's."

"True." And I'm not about to split the work with anybody else and let them cut in on my payday. "It's okay. I can handle it. It'll just take a good part of the day."

"Let me know if you run into any problems." Now that she knows I'll take care of the job, she's all light and breezy.

"You mean, if I open the wrong closet door and find dead bodies hanging from hooks?"

"Lisa told me she cleaned those up last time, and he has promised he'd never leave them out again."

I gulp the rest of my coffee. It's already cold. "Famous last words."

CHAPTER 2

Dani

"Holy. Mother. Of God!" I gasp, throwing the door open.

I'm too intimidated at first to even step through the front door. I've never seen anything like this before. Normally, I clean homes around North Jersey, the sort of places one would expect mobsters like the ones on TV to live in. Maybe they do, I don't know. I never see the owners. I'm always there while the house is empty, as though the home's owners don't want to risk exposure to the person who cleans up after them. It might break some fragile cosmic balance.

But nothing I've seen in those McMansions can touch what stretches out before me.

One person needs all this space?

I don't take my eyes off the living room as I stretch the

plastic covers over my sneakers, then pick up the caddy which holds my cleaning tools—including the required cleaning solvents and two brand-new toothbrushes for cleaning the grout in the showers. One room, one toothbrush.

Yeah, unreal.

But then, the entire situation is unreal or close to it. In a daze, I walk through the door and close it behind me. I can't help but forget about the cleaning for a moment as I walk straight to the plate-glass windows which stretch from one end of the large, open room to the other and look out over half of New York. I'm so high up, the people down in the park look like ants.

I can barely think straight, it's all so beautiful. I can't help but remember the girl I used to be—still am in a deep, secret part of my heart. The girl who only wore the hand-me-downs of strangers. Granted, I'm only in this apartment because I'm supposed to clean it. I don't live here. It's not mine and it never will be.

But I'm here. That's something, anyway.

"Oh, hell." I catch my reflection in the window, the curve-hugging tank top under a bleach-splotched hoodie, the yoga pants and covered sneakers, and I realize I haven't covered my hair yet. I couldn't find a hairnet so I just bought a shower cap. I pull my long, chocolate locks into a high pony-tail and stuff it into the cap while rolling my eyes. What a weirdo this guy must be.

He has taste, though. I'll give him that.

I would never know how to begin decorating a place this big, this exquisite. The dark, polished wood floors gleam in the clear light flooding through the windows. The sleek leather furniture could be mistaken for art pieces.

I look around for photos, but there are none. Not surprising, considering the list of dos and don'ts I've got tucked into my pocket. He probably considers all other people unhygienic. It must be hard to have sex with a woman while she is wearing a hair net and shoe covers.

There's a long bar along one side of the room, fully stocked. Black leather bar stools line up before it. A glass-enclosed fireplace makes it possible to enjoy a cozy fire from both the living room and formal dining room, with its long table and many chairs. The center piece is an intricate glass sculpture.

Every room is like this, I realize as I take a brief tour.

I could probably hide out in this place and the owner would never find me. It's that big. There's a greenhouse with a glass roof and hundreds of plants. A chef's kitchen that looks like it has never been used. There is even a butler pantry. The media room, complete with reclining chairs that face a massive flat screen panel. Just when I thought I knew everything about this cold ordered house, I come across a popcorn machine that I'm just aching to test out. Better not. Something tells me my client would clue into the scent of popcorn in the air.

I can't waste time forever, so I pop in my earbuds and start up an audiobook on personal development. Some people work to music, and I can completely relate to that, but I find that listening to a guru as they urge me to take control of my life and climb toward a better future is particularly inspiring when I'm scrubbing a toilet.

It won't be like this forever.

Hours pass with Antony Robinson whispering in my ear. By the time I finish toothbrushing the grout, washing and polishing the hardwood floors of the entire first floor by hand, and using an extendable duster to reach the corners between the walls and fifteen-foot ceilings, my back, shoulders and knees are killing me.

And I still have to do the second floor.

At least two of the rooms are unused guest rooms, and one of the bathrooms is also unused. I wipe that one down with my spray bottle of vinegar and lemon—he's so generous, letting me get away with only wiping the room down—before changing the linens.

Even unused, they must be changed. Who is this person?

I notice Lisa's attention to detail when it came to hospital corners and I make a mental note to do the same, even as the wicked voice in the back of my mind tells me he'd never know if I change the sheets or not. They haven't even been slept in, and all the others in the linen closet are exactly the same.

But a sane little voice in my head says he'll know. I don't even know who this crusty old dude is, but I just know in my bones, he'll know.

By the time I'm finished with everything but the master bedroom and bathroom suite, it's been seven hours and I can't even get excited about the money because holy crap, I'm going to die of exhaustion. Wouldn't that be ironic? Killing myself to make his apartment perfectly clean? Then dying in the middle of it, lying there for two days? Mr. Demanding would probably move out.

I text Helen to let her know I'm finished because damn it, I need a short break, but I don't feel right relaxing on the client's dime. I'll do these last two rooms off the clock—after all, a thousand dollars minus Helen's ten percent is nothing to sneeze at. For me, it's nearly half a month of work. I can almost pay the rent on my little Red Bank studio apartment or the entire month's bills. Maybe I can take a little time to focus on my schoolwork. As exhausting as this day has been, it's also been a godsend. I can't pretend it hasn't.

The fact that the bed is so huge and so darn comfy looking isn't helping. All right. I'll do the bathroom, then take a break before changing the bed and dusting everything. It's a very masculine suite—the entire apartment is masculine, but this even more so. I can't quite put my finger on it. I'd know in a heartbeat that this room belongs to a man.

The bathroom, with its sunken marble tub large enough for four people, heated floors and ten-jet shower is my idea of heaven. It is also roughly the size of my entire apartment. If it were mine, I would never leave. I'd just soak in the tub until my skin pruned and eventually fell off entirely. I'd be that deeply committed.

Another hour and another room finished. He's a neat freak, for sure. His toiletries are lined up perfectly, and they're all ultra-expensive brands in sleek, sexy packaging. I'm such a sucker for things like that. A salesperson's dream come true.

It's six o'clock now and I've been cleaning for seven hours. I need a rest. I look longingly at the big bed. I have to change the sheets anyway, so it won't matter if I take a tiny little rest at the foot of the bed, will it? I sure hope not, because oh, look, I'm already sinking down onto it and the silk slides against my bare arms, and I'm more comfortable than I've been in a long time. My entire body is singing right now.

Singing a lullaby.

My eyelids slide shut.

CHAPTER 3

Brock

"Truthfully, I don't give a damn what you tell them. They don't deserve an explanation. They weren't there on time. I don't wait for anyone. They can fly up to New York to see me if they really want this deal."

"But, Mr. Garret—"

"Are you questioning my decision, Sarah?" I ask, my voice bristling with impatience.

"No, of course, not," Sarah gasps, horrified to have pissed me off. "I'm sorry, sir. My only concern is for you."

A twinge of guilt touches my heart. She's a kind soul and old enough to be my grandmother. She should be treated a little gentler than the many PAs who've come and gone over the years. There were times when it felt like they were coming in through a revolving door. They were in and out so quickly.

One of them lasted all of two hours. One moment she was trying to get my coffee order correctly, the next, she fled out of the doors in tears.

But not Sarah.

She's hung in with me for the last 2 years, is excellent at her job, and shows no signs of going anywhere. I've even started to rely on her, which would make it extremely unfortunate if she left.

"I realize that, Sarah…I shouldn't have been so sharp, and I'm sorry." I'm rarely in the wrong, but admitting when I am, has never been a problem for me.

"I completely understand, sir. I'll tell the investors that you had an emergency at home which needed attending to immediately."

"Tell them whatever makes you feel happy."

"Thank you, sir."

"It's extremely late. Shouldn't you have left the office hours ago?"

"You know how it is, sir. There's nothing for me at home but my cats, and half the time, they act as though they were happier before I got home."

I chuckle, though I do wish I could do something more for her than giving her a salary that puts her in the category of most highly paid PA in the world. She's too valuable a person, and not just an assistant, but a person, to be left living alone with her cats. Funny thing is she doesn't strike me as a cat lady. Her clothing is always impeccably free of hair. Lucky her, because I'm allergic to cats, dogs, birds, reptiles, people…

"Right. Good night, Sarah. See you at work tomorrow."

"Have a safe trip, sir."

I hang up with a slight smile, satisfied in the knowledge that there will never be repercussions as a result of doing as I damn well please. The unfathomably solid returns I've generated over the past seven quarters for Garret Industries has become a phenomenon. The kind that's gotten my picture on the cover of every financial magazine since I took over what used to be a struggling parts manufacturer and turned it around.

I lean back against the leather seats of the car carrying me towards the airplane hangar where my jet is housed. To be honest, I'm actually glad I'm leaving LA two days early.

I could never understand why it's such a big draw for people. I hate it. Sure, the weather's nice, but underneath the glitz, glamour, and tanned bodies, it's just hollow. New York is much more my speed. Sophisticated and stylish, but gritty. Real. Willing to come to blows if need be and crack open a beer once the fight is over.

My phone buzzes.

"Are you sitting down?" my best friend, Mark asks.

I frown. "Yes. Why?"

"Charlotte is getting married."

"Why do I need to be sitting down for that? I'm not the poor bastard she's marrying."

"I don't know. I thought it might affect you. It looked like a difficult breakup."

Yeah. It was difficult. For her. She miscalculated. She thought she could bring me to heel if I thought other men wanted her. I told her they were welcome to her. The day I'd walked into my apartment and found her spread-eagled on the bed with another man on top of her flashed into my head. Her shocked face, when I said, "Carry on. Finish." I had the place fumigated after that. The screaming and crying, the swearing of how she loved me and would never hurt me again. What a load of bullshit. As if I cared. She did me a fucking favor.

"You still there?" Mark asks.

"Yeah."

"So anyway, she called me not five minutes ago to announce that she's marrying this guy in Vegas this weekend. I didn't even know she was seeing him until, like, two weeks ago."

My driver opens my door and I get out, walking towards my jet. "I wasn't aware that the two of you stayed in touch."

"I wouldn't call it staying in touch. She texts or phones every once in a while to tell me how amazing her life is. I always assumed she expected me to take the information back to you, so obviously, I never did. Why would I give her what she wants?"

I nod at the captain, and run lightly up the steps.

She was hot, fun to be with and great in bed. That deserved to be acknowledged, too. Her magic trick needed a pack of condoms and a male volunteer.

"You still there?" Mark asked, raising his voice over the noise around me.

"Yeah. Still here."

"You know she wasn't right for you. Let's be honest, she's not the forever type. You know that, right? Women like her, who needs them."

"I know."

"It's your pride that cares more than anything else."

I cut him off there. "Why do I get the impression you think this bit of news has devastated me?"

"Hasn't it?" he mumbles.

"Fuck no."

"Uh, there's something else."

"You're fucking kidding me. What else is there?" I checked my watch, and pick up the glass of freshly squeezed tomato juice, the air stewardess places in front of me.

"You're gonna laugh. I swear to God, you're gonna laugh."

"I wouldn't bet the farm on that, bro."

"She asked me to be the best man."

I nearly choke on the juice. "You're shitting me."

"Nope."

"And you said?"

"Yes."

"I thought you said you didn't even know she was dating this guy until recently."

"I didn't. I've never met him."

"So why?"

"Ah, man. You know I've always had a thing for her friend. She's going to be maid of honor and you know how closely the maid of honor has to work with the best man."

I laugh. "Well, she sure knows where everybody's buttons are."

"I guess it's the ultimate revenge, huh? Asking your best friend to stand up at her wedding."

"Actually, it doesn't bother me at all."

"Still, what kind of guy allows the best friend of his ex to be his best man? She must have his balls in her purse, man. I wonder what she offered in return for this?"

I didn't have to wonder. I know. A man doesn't forget the kind of things Charlotte Leyton is willing to do to keep a man coming back for more. I guess that must have been one long night for her.

"Look, if you mind, or prefer I don't do it, I'll say no," Mark offers.

"Mind? No, I don't mind. Go ahead and have a great time. Bang the maid of honor. Fuck the bride for all I care."

Mark chuckles. "Yeah, I'll try. Bang the maid of honor, I mean. Uh…one more thing."

"What?"

He gives a bark of forced laughter. "Umm…Charlotte wants to ask you to come, but doesn't have the nerve." Mark saved the best for last.

Doesn't have the nerve? Clearly, Mark has no idea what Charlotte is made of. "I've never heard anything so ridiculous."

"I know. I felt the same way, but I promised I'd pass on the invite, just the same."

"Thanks, I'll pass," I say, marveling at Mark's naivety. Charlotte is easily one of the most cunning and manipulative women I have ever had the misfortune to meet. She's just dangled a carrot in front of Mark so he'd do all the donkey work for her.

"But it could be fun, huh? Las Vegas. We could burn some money together, maybe get smashed and get laid," Mark suggests excitedly.

There, he just did her dirty work for her.

"No offence, but I'd rather sit in a dentist's chair for two hours, than be within a mile of Charlotte again."

"Anyway, we can talk more about it when you get back," Mark says hopefully. "I'll be waiting with a couple of beers by the time you get there."

"Yeah, man. Will do. Talk soon." I hang up without telling him I was coming back tonight.

CHAPTER 4

Brock

"Sir?" The driver's voice stirs me out of my thoughts, and I realize we've stopped in front of my building. I look up at the tall grey structure. Home never looked so good. It's a pleasure to unfold my long body and step out of the car.

I draw in a deep breath. New York. It smells of traffic, food carts, the crush of 27,000 people per square mile, the garbage they produce, and naked ambition. It's not a good smell but it's honest. Yes, I appreciate this city in a way I can never appreciate LA.

The lobby staff is gracious as always as I stride through. I catch a glimpse of myself in the mirrored walls of the elevator, and notice the worry lines around my normally clear, blue eyes. They seem soulless and cynical. Is there really nothing more than just this? Have I hit the peak and not realized?

I put my key in my door. I need to be alone for a little while. Recharge my batteries. There hasn't been a day created yet that couldn't be amended by opening my front door and knowing that everything is just the way I left it, just the way I like it. I look around at the grand space. Maybe there is nothing more, but maybe this is enough.

"Home." I take in a deep breath.

This is my sanctuary. My haven. My solitude and peace in a fast moving, uncaring world. My first stop is the bar along one side of the living room. The bottles are gleaming, which tells me the cleaner has been around and gone. Good thing, since I'd hate to walk in on her and take great pains to make sure I don't. Privacy is sacred in my world. Maybe because I got so little of it for so much of my life.

I pour out a small measure of Scotch. I know better than to overindulge. I know what that can do and never want it to happen to me. One of the overarching themes of my life: refraining from overindulgence. I take a sip of the drink made from a half-a-century old barrel of whiskey, and savor the smooth, mellow burn. Carrying the glass, I move through my home.

The apartment looks good. Whoever cleaned it did a solid job. Everything looks better than normal, I realize. The floors shine brighter than usual. The windows seem cleaner. The scent of lemon oil fills the air.

Is it a new girl?

There's one way to know. I jog upstairs to one of the two guest bedrooms. I pull up the corner of the mattress. What I find surprises me. *Yup. It's a new girl.* None of the others have ever bothered to change the sheets.

My discovery is enough to make me take a good look around the room, then around the second floor. I'll have to ask Sarah to call the service and offer my approval and order that they never assign another cleaner, ever. This one is perfect, whoever she is.

Now, I'm softly humming to myself as I loosen my tie and walk down the hall to my bedroom. A hot shower is what today calls for.

No, a hard workout, then a shower.

I step through the doorway and the sight on my bed makes me stop short, almost sloshing Scotch out of the glass and onto the freshly-polished floor. No, scratch that. The floor hasn't been polished yet. It doesn't have the same gleam as the floor in the hall.

What the fuck? The cleaner is fast asleep on my bed!

She stopped and took a goddamned nap on my bed.

No commendation for this one.

Who the hell does she think she is? Curled up like a sleeping cat on my bedspread. I hope she doesn't think I'm paying her to take a fucking nap. How long has she been staying here? Has she done this before? I'm already striding over to the bed and ready to give her the wakeup she deserves when she rolls onto her back, revealing her face for the first time.

I freeze with shock.

Is it her? Could it be? Jesus Christ, how long has it been since I last saw her? At least ten years. No, more like eleven or twelve. People change a lot over that long a stretch of time, especially when it's the stretch between childhood and adulthood.

Even so, it's her. I'm as sure of it as I am of my birthday. It has to be her. The color of her hair escaping from her shower cap. Her full mouth and brows. Her high cheekbones and slightly dimpled chin. The tiny mole beside her right eye, almost unnoticeable until a person looks close enough.

Yes. It's Dani. Dani Saber.

If I believed in God or a Higher Power, I'd swear the girl was dropped into *my* bed by such power. It's enough to make a person believe in fate, if nothing else. Because this is the girl I've never been able to forget, not after all these years, and all the willing women.

Wherever her life has taken her it has thrown her right back into my path. Forget path. In my goddamn bed! It's the most incredible, unbelievable, impossible thing. I couldn't have predicted this in my wildest dreams. I'm not the one who gets thrown off my game. Not me. But, I can feel my wild excitement racing through my blood.

I can't lose my cool.

I need to think about this. How should I handle the situation? It's strange for me, not knowing immediately what to do. I trust my instincts implicitly, always have. Nobody knows what's better for me than me. But this? This is a whole other ballgame.

She doesn't budge or even flutter her eyelids.

She's obviously exhausted. Because of me? I hate the idea of her working herself to that level of exhaustion. She's grown up well. Full in the hips, the ass, the tits. Slim waist and legs. I feel my cock stir for all her delectable curves. Hell, I want to exhaust her in other ways. So many other ways.

I step quickly and quietly out of the room and walk in a daze thought my vast apartment.

I go into the kitchen and stand, staring down at the breath-taking view of the city below me, but I can't stop picturing the woman in my bed. Imagining her on the counter, legs around my waist.

It was so many years ago. Yet, it is fresh in mind as if it were only yesterday. I try to superimpose the image of the woman upstairs over the image of that scared, brave little girl in the schoolyard.

The one selling kisses...

CHAPTER 5

Dani
(Twelve years ago)

I carry my Kisses = $1 sign into the schoolyard and lean it against a wooden bench. I made it very pretty, by painting one corner with two pink love hearts, and decorating the other with a yellow flower.

I stand an old cookie tin next to it. That's for collecting all the money.

A sudden blast of icy cold wind makes me feel as if my teeth are about to start chattering. The zip of my jacket is busted so I pull the ends tighter around my neck, but it's so thin it makes no difference.

I wish I could be like that beautiful lady I saw on TV. She was selling kisses from her booth at the Funfair. Laughing and flicking her long blonde hair back while calling out to the men to come to her. But I'm so nervous my stomach feels like there are butterflies flying around.

What if no one wants my kisses?

When I see some kids point at my sign and start walking towards me, I quickly smooth my hands over my chocolate brown hair. It's not blonde, but it's shiny and smells good because I washed it last night. Even I know nobody wants to buy kisses from a girl with horrid hair.

If only it wasn't so chilly, I wouldn't need my jacket. It makes me look poor. I know that. Mom says she'll take me to the charity store to get another one soon, but she's been sick a lot this fall and I don't want to bother her. Anyway, I hate going to the charity shop. All the clothes there stink of armpits.

It would be really nice if we could buy things from a real store, but Mom says we can't afford them. Dad doesn't work anymore and there's never any money because he drinks away what little we have. Before I started sticking cotton balls in my ears so I could get some sleep, I used to hear them fighting. Or he would shout and she would cry. Really hard.

Mom says it's easier for him to drink and feel happy than it is to face up to what his life is really like. I think that's stupid. His life stinks because he drinks like he does, and he can't keep a job because he's always drunk. Then he spends what little money we have on beer and whiskey.

It's pretty obvious to me what he should do. He should stop drinking. But what do I know? I'm only eleven and grown-ups don't listen to you until you're at least twelve.

When I grow up, I'm never going to drink. Not ever.

Especially now, that I know it can make a grown man cry. Like Dad did last night.

Hugging my younger brother and me, he sobbed about how sorry he was for the water stains on the ceiling, our crummy little house, and the carpet that's so worn down you can see the stuff underneath that holds it all together.

I told him it didn't matter. No matter what happens, I'll love him forever.

He hugged me and said I was the best daughter in the whole world.

When he said that I cried too. I told him I loved him to the moon and back. I even lied and said I didn't care that we're poor. I know it would hurt him to know that the kids always make fun of me for being poor.

But not the boys who are starting to gather in front of me. They're not making fun of me right now, even though some of them are the ones who usually do. Today, right now, they're looking at me with interest. It seems as if they like me enough that they all have a dollar to give me for kissing them. I do a quick count.

Fifteen boys. Wow! Fifteen dollars!

I know it isn't enough to get me a brand-new jacket, or buy anything important, but I could maybe get a couple of boxes of macaroni and cheese for dinner tonight, and a little milk to make it with. It would help Mom, and it would mean she wouldn't have to cry when she makes us eat peanut butter and jelly sandwiches again.

Until a month ago, Mom used to take food out of the super-market dumpster. I know it sounds disgusting, but the food wasn't rotting or anything. The supermarket throws out loads of perfectly good stuff all the time. Meat, vegetables, bread, fruit. Even ice-cream. We have to freeze it back again, of course, but it doesn't matter because it tastes just as good.

We used to have really good food then. Mom used to make all kinds of tasty meals with what she found in the bins.

But one night, the security guard caught her doing it, and now they lock all their bins. Dad says it's the stupid regulations in this country, but I don't understand why they would do that. Why would they want to throw it away when we are starving? Actually, I'm really worried about Mom's health. I don't want her to become even skinnier.

Still, if this works, I could do it tomorrow and the day after that…

"How much for a kiss?" Robbie snickers. He's in my class and he's stupid.

I try not to roll my eyes as I point to my sign where it clearly lists the price. "A dollar."

"How much to show us your boobs?" he asks with his stupid laugh.

Some of the boys snicker and look sly, and the girls who are standing around in groups look like they have just smelled their own stinky farts.

I know they think I'm a slut or whatever for doing this. They don't understand, but it doesn't matter what they think. They're all mean, anyway. They're even mean to each other which I don't understand. They're supposed to be friends. I wouldn't want to be friends with somebody who was mean to me, even when they were smiling. They're not smiling right now. They're muttering things to each other and shaking their heads, and wrinkling their noses the way they do when they see the food I bring for lunch every day. They're the reason why I eat in the stairwell now.

Suddenly, I don't feel good anymore. I feel sick. Dad taught me a long time ago, when I was really little and he didn't drink as much as he does now, that if there was ever something that gave me a sick little feeling in my stomach, that it was my inside voice telling me what I was going to do was a bad thing.

My inside voice would always know, he told me, even if the people around me were all daring me and telling me it would be okay. All I need to do is check in with my stomach and see what it thought. So, my stomach is telling me this isn't right, but I want our family to sit down to a macaroni dinner tonight.

I glare at Robbie and jut my chin out angrily. "Don't be so stupid. This is a kissing booth."

"I'll go first," Zack announces, stepping forward. He's in my class too, and he's always so pushy, but he has a dollar and I need that dollar.

I nod and tell my stomach to shut up because you know what's worse than butterflies flying around telling you you're doing something wrong. When your stomach is empty because there is no food at all for dinner, and you have to go to bed and hope sleep comes fast, so you don't have to feel hungry anymore.

I take his dollar and put it into my tin. When I look up, all the boys are pushing and shoving to get in line behind him.

I take a deep breath and nod at him.

Zack leans forward.

I close my eyes when he presses his lips to mine. It doesn't take long and he smells of chocolate, so that's good. When it's over, he gives me the dollar and walks away smiling proudly.

I make a big deal of smiling too and acting like this doesn't bother me at all, as I wave the next boy forward. Now that I know how to, I kiss him really fast to get it over with, and move my head back.

As I turn to put the dollar into my tin, I feel someone watching me.

It is a boy. He's wearing a leather jacket and blue jeans and he is leaning against the wall of the school building, his arms crossed over his chest. And oh, my gosh! He's so handsome it's freaky. His dark hair is so thick and perfect. Blue eyes. I've seen boys like him on TV and I've always wondered what it would be like to see one in person.

I can feel him staring at me as I kiss the next boy. I don't know if I should look at him, or pretend that he's not even alive. I know I shouldn't but I can't help looking over at him as the kiss ends.

The next boy steps up as I'm staring at the boy across the schoolyard. I can't tell if he's just interested in watching, or he wants to come over and get in line. I can feel the skin on the back of my neck get all prickly when I think about what it would be like to kiss him.

He's so, so cute.

But I have to think about the boy standing in front of me, so

I turn and look at him. And my heart sinks a little. He's not in my grade, and I don't know his name, but I know him by sight. Everybody does. It's hard to miss him. He wears thick glasses, weighs a million pounds, and has a mouth full of ugly metal braces. I don't want to kiss him.

But he has a dollar. I can see it in his hand, sort of crumpled up.

My eyes swivel over to the handsome boy. He's still standing there, just watching, and my cheeks start to burn. I wish he wouldn't watch this part. What's he going to think of me? He looks older, a lot older, like the fat boy in front of me. Maybe they're in the same grade. I would die. I would just die. Why can't he go away? Or if he's going to hang around, why doesn't he get in line?

I want to be kissing him. Not the boy in front of me. I can't help it but suddenly, burning tears come into my eyes. I can't stop them. They roll down my face. I'm so ashamed, I want to crawl into a hole and die.

And he sees it, the boy in front of me.

I know he must think I'm crying because of him being who he is, but really, I'm not. I'm crying because I shouldn't be kissing all these boys. I'm crying because I know Dad won't like it if he knew—because I wish I could be like all the other girls and only kiss the boys I like.

Even through my tears I see his face fall and I start feel bad for him too. I know how he feels. He must get teased a lot for being fat just like I get teased for my clothes and the food I eat. He frowns and looks at the ground, and now I feel worse, so I start crying for real. Big, hot tears that roll quickly down my cheeks and drip onto my stupid, worthless jacket. I know I should stop, but I can't.

Then, the fat boy does something odd. He reaches into his jeans and pulls out a bunch of money all crumpled up, and shoves it into my cold palm. "Go home," he says.

"Huh?" I hiccup.

"Go home." He doesn't say anything else.

I don't need him to, anyway. I have all this money, and there's no way I can face everybody in school again today. Maybe not ever again. I just want to die. I take off at a run and I hear the kids still waiting in line grumble and curse because they didn't get their turn.

I hear something else, too, as I run past the wall where the handsome boy is. I hear him calling out to me.

"Hey, kid!"

But I can't look back. Not at him. I'm so ashamed. All I can do is run with the money clenched in my fist as tight as I can hold it to be sure I don't lose it. I run all the way home.

I didn't have to worry about going to that school again, anyway.

The next morning, some people from Child Protection Services come to the house. They bring two policemen with them. They say they received complaints that I was selling my body in the school yard. They speak sternly to my parents, and throw around words like unfit parents, stealing food from the dumpster, and foster families.

They speak to me gently and tell me they're taking me away to live with another family.

Mom screams hysterically at Dad to do something. He puts his head in his hands and cries, but he doesn't tell them to get out of our house.

I tell them I don't want to go, but they drag me away kicking and screaming.

CHAPTER 6

Brock
(Present Day)

I never saw her again after that day, but we all heard the stories.

Even at my young age, I understood why she was selling her kisses in the first place. The girls called her a slut and a skank, even though they didn't really understand what they were saying.

But I knew better.

I don't know her now and didn't back then either, but I've always had a way of reading people. The poor kid was just trying to help out her family the best way she knew how.

One night while I was doing homework with my bedroom door open I overheard my parents mention the Saber family. I crept to the top of the stairs and listened to them discussing her drunken, worthless father and her sick mother.

Both died within two years of Dani and her brother being removed from the home. I used to wonder if she knew. I even hoped that she'd come back for the funerals. Just so I could see her again, and know she was doing all right.

I've had to wait twelve years for this day.

But what the hell has happened to her? She's fucking cleaning houses for a living. It's better than a lot of things she could be doing, but not nearly good enough for her.

I look up the stairs. The white marble shines under the lights. She must have got down on her hands and knees to do them. Something in my chest hurts.

There was always something special about her. She had guts. She was determined and strong, not to mention resourceful. And she was the most beautiful girl I'd ever set eyes on. She never knew, but I used to watch her. Back then, I was crazy about her. I used to write her name in my notebooks. Once, I even punched another kid for saying something nasty about her. Got a temporary suspension, and my dad was mad as hell with me, but it'd been worth it.

I guess I've always had a thing for her.

Funny how life hinges on meaningless little decisions. Stay in bed a few minutes longer and miss the train that crashes. Take your kid in for his first day of school and avoid being in the office when a plane hits the building. If my investors had arrived on time I would have stayed on in LA for another two days and I would never have met her again.

I take the stairs more slowly this time, and quieter than

before. She needs her sleep. I wonder what she'd think if she knew who I was. Here I am, getting all sentimental over her, when I doubt she'll even remember me.

Back in the bedroom, where she's still deeply asleep, I settle comfortably into a chair across from her, and watch her sleeping. I need a plan, a solid plan. Before she wakes up.

Her breathing is soft and light, even. Her mouth curves into a slight smile and I wonder what she's dreaming of. Or of whom. My body clenches at the thought. My eyes fly down to her fingers. No ring on her left hand. A good sign.

When the idea hits, it's like a bolt from the blue.

It's still sketchy, still in its early stages, but it's the ideal way to keep her in my life. Because I must. I must keep her with me now. There's no other option. I'd be a foolish man to let her slip away from me again. Opportunities like this don't come around more than once in a lifetime.

I slide my phone from my pants and text Mark.

ME: Slight change of plans. Tell Charlotte I'm coming to Vegas for her wedding.

His return text comes through almost instantly. *Awesome. We'll have a blast.*

ME: BTW, I'm bringing my fiancée.

MARK: WTF???!!!

I smile. *Tell you when I see you later tonight.*

MARK: Tonight? Aren't you in LA?

ME: Nope. See you about nine.

MARK: *Can't wait to hear this story.*

I glance away from the screen and over to Dani.

She stirs as if she feels my gaze, or knows what I'm thinking as she sleeps.

Wouldn't it be something if I showed up in Vegas with her on my arm? Poor Charlotte. I'll try my hardest not to rub it in, but she can only dream of being like Dani.

I sit there for a while, watching her from my chair as she sleeps. Planning. Wondering. Looking forward to the moment when my Sleeping Beauty awakens.

CHAPTER 7

Dani

Oh, wow! I've *never* been so comfortable. Never in my whole life.

As I slowly work my way back to consciousness, I become aware of everything around me. The cool silk bedspread is just as incredible on my skin as it was before I fell asleep. I've worked my way into the mattress and I'm pretty sure I'll never be able to get back up. Not when it cradles me, fits around my body like a glove.

I think it's made of clouds. That's got to be it. I just slept on a cloud. And darn it, I might fall back to sleep just for the hell of it. Because when am I ever going to have a chance to sleep on a bed like this again?

Slowly—oh, so slowly—something else works its way into my senses. A scent I haven't noticed throughout the time I've been inside this amazing penthouse. Hmmm…a musky, spicy scent.

As I hone in on it, other sensations start filtering through. The sound of breathing—that isn't coming from me.

My eyes fly open with shock, and I'm greeted by the sight of the most drop-dead gorgeous man I've ever seen. He is sitting in a leather club chair across from where I'm curled up at the foot of the bed. One ankle is crossed over the other knee and his long fingers are tented beneath his chin. His startling blue eyes are trained directly on me.

Oh. My. God.

"I'm so sorry!" I scramble off the bed and to my feet. My cheeks are burning with shame like I've never known. Shame and guilt. And the knowledge that there's no way he's going to pay me for all the work I've done after walking in and finding me asleep on his bed. The man made me toothbrush his already-clean grout. I don't think he's the type to forgive something like this.

What's worse, he doesn't say a word. He just looks at me with an inscrutable expression. His finely-drawn mouth neither frowning nor smiling. His square jaw isn't clenched but is tight, which tells me he's not pleased. Something's bothering him, regardless of whether or not it's me he's displeased with.

Wait, what the hell am I thinking?

Of course, it's me. He's just found me sleeping in his bed, like I'm Goldilocks, or something even though I'm not a blonde, and he's not a bear. Though he is pretty big and I'm pretty sure he could tear me to pieces if he wanted to.

"Truly, I'm sorry for this. I cleaned for seven hours and I was up all night studying and—and I was just so exhausted, and you weren't supposed to be back for two days. I was going to change the sheets, anyway. So it's not like I've done any real harm—I'm sorry. I shouldn't have said that. Of course, it was wrong, germs and all that."

His eyebrows shoot up, though he remains silent.

"I apologize. I tend to babble when I'm scared to death and I'm scared right now, because I really need the money from this job and oh, look, I'm babbling again."

He holds up a hand to signal silence.

Instantly, my mouth snaps shut.

He's still staring, which I would tell him is just about the most unnerving thing in the entire world if he hadn't already signaled for me to shut up.

My insides are all quaky and shaky and a little watery. What's he going to do to me? Call Helen? Get me fired? Oh, my God, I need this job. I'll even give him today's work as a freebie if he promises not to get me fired.

"What's your name?"

My eyes widen. Interesting lead-in. "Dani. Dani Saber," I whisper cautiously.

He nods. "Dani. I assume you're not the usual cleaning woman who takes care of my apartment."

Crap again and again. How did he find out? Did I miss a spot or something? Is he going to get angrier if he finds out I'm not his regular? But Helen didn't say it was secret. I should just come clean since he probably already knows, seeing he brought the issue up. Lying would definitely be a bad move. I nod with a sigh. "That's right. How did you know?" I can't help but ask. I know I was as thorough as I could be.

"You changed the linens in the guest rooms."

My jaw drops in shock. "Hang on. Lisa doesn't normally change the linens?"

"Not unless there's evidence of the bed having been used since she was last here."

I shake my head in wonder. "But how can you tell? All the sheets are exactly the same."

"The inside corner of each sheet is embroidered with a different color. Call it extreme, but I like to know what my cleaning people are up to."

I nod, even more impressed at the extent of his weirdness. "Why didn't you ever say anything?"

He shrugs. "Your service is the only one I've found so far that's anywhere close to suitable. Otherwise, your coworker does an adequate job. You, however, do excellent work, and I always give credit where credit is due."

"Thank you so much," I breathe out, some of the tension draining out of me.

"Except for the part where you fell asleep on my bed, rather than completing the job."

And the tension is back. "I know. As I said and say again, I'm sorry. Very, very sorry. Please don't tell Helen, I mean, Mrs. Lincoln."

He ignores everything I said and asks me a totally different question, "You said you were up studying all night?"

I frown. "Until four in the morning." Which reminds me. I look around. "What time is it now?"

"Ten-thirty," he murmurs without checking his Rolex.

Ten-thirty? Jesus, I didn't take a nap. I had half a night's sleep. "Again, I'm so very sorry. I won't take long to finish up in here. An hour tops. If you want to wait downstairs, I'll be as quick as I can."

"No," he says quietly.

Did he just say no? "Oh, all right then. I'll come back tomorrow when you are at work, or something."

He has a very powerful personality, for sure. I know I should be afraid of him, or at least intimidated. The hair stands up on the back of my neck whenever our eyes meet, like he's shooting invisible electric sparks at me. It's a sort of intoxicating sensation, and damn it, he's toe-curlingly, gloriously hot. Easily the best-looking person I've seen.

What can I say?

I've always appreciated beauty. I let my eyes side away from his sculptured mouth and begin to walk backwards. Even though I don't actually want to be out of his way. "Okay. I should be off. I'm sorry again. And thank you. Bye now."

I'm two seconds away from the door when his commanding voice stops me in my tracks. "Not so fast."

CHAPTER 8

Dani

My stomach drops. "Excuse me?"

"I said, not so fast. Are you hard of hearing?"

Oh, so that's it. I'm still sleeping and this is some bizarre dream. Is it possible for a person to hallucinate after inhaling too much vinegar and lemon? "My hearing is just fine. I was only wondering why you would order me around like that."

"I *asked* you because there are other things I wish to discuss with you. When it's time for you to work in my bedroom, you'll be the first to know."

My skin flushes and there's the hair on the back of my neck standing up again, right on schedule. Does he even know he dropped a heavy double entendre? Yes. I think he does. My cheeks burn even hotter than before. I'll just ignore that. "What is it you want to discuss?"

"Have a seat." He gestures toward the bed.

I shouldn't just give in, but it's probably better for me to just do things without asking why, even if it runs counter to my personality. One of the things that always drove my foster mother crazy was the way I couldn't stop asking questions. She liked it a lot better when I kept my mouth shut.

I perch carefully, only slightly unnerved by the way he's staring at me. "Did anybody ever tell you it's rude to stare?" I murmur.

"I can't help it. I've never seen that shade of red on a human face before." For the first time, a slight smile plays at the corners of his mouth.

—Oh, my Lord, it's possible for him to be even sexier. Pure lust explodes inside my body. He's superhuman, or an angel, or something. That has to be it. I press my palms to my burning face. "What is it, then? I'm sure you want to unwind after traveling."

"I'm fine, thank you." He straightens out his long legs.

I can't help but notice how thick with muscle they are. He's a real piece of work, in many ways. My eyes helplessly stray upwards, past the area of his—umm—upper-thighs and just a little bit higher, and oh, my—that is some package he has there. Big. Suddenly, I realize what I'm doing and lift my eyes all the way up to his, and they are sparkling with wicked humor.

Oh, God. So embarrassing.

He just watched me check out his junk, and I was practically drooling. I'm such a dumbass. I should just suffocate myself on his super-soft pillows right now. If my cheeks were red before I cannot imagine what color they must be now. They feel like they're on fire. I meet his amused gaze for a split second before letting them jerk away, while I desperately think of something to say, but really, what can I say? It was an eye-lick pure and simple.

He gestures next to his head with his finger. "Can you remove that thing on your head?"

Jesus, can this get any worse? "Oh." I snatch the shower cap away and my hair tumbles untidily down over my shoulders and back.

His eyes darken as he looks at me through half-lidded eyes. "Hmmm…"

I shift awkwardly. "What do you mean 'hmmm'?"

"I have a problem which I believe you can help me with."

My heart starts hammering in my chest. I still haven't forgotten his comment about *working* in his bedroom. Is he going to proposition me? Does he think I'm that type of girl? Well, I was sleeping in his bed. A thousand thoughts fly through my head at the speed of light. *Dani, you are one sex-starved, pitifully pathetic woman! What should I do?* This time, I decide, I need to say something. "I hope you don't think I'm going to do anything with you…"

His eyes flash. "I'm insulted you'd even think such a thing."

I can feel myself start blushing again. Like a freak. I lift my chin defiantly. "I don't know you. How would I know what you're thinking?"

His gorgeous eyes give me a lazy once over. "I don't need to offer women money for sex, Dani."

"That's good to know."

"I'm offering you a trip to Las Vegas."

"Excuse me?"

"There you are again, asking me to excuse you. In which way was I unclear?"

I tip my head to the side. "When you offered a stranger a trip to Las Vegas. Somewhere around there."

"Allow me to explain," he says, a slow smile is tugging his mouth upwards. He leans forward, elbows on his knees, his stare intense. Like he can see through my clothes.

I realize for the first time that I'm only wearing my tank top. The hoodie got discarded hours and hours ago, once the work got a little tougher. I resist the urge to cross my arms over my cleavage.

"I have a wedding to attend in Las Vegas, and it's unfortunately the wedding of my ex-girlfriend."

"Oh." My nose wrinkles. "That's no good."

"That's putting it mildly. I've been dreading it ever since the happy event was announced. We only broke up a few months ago, after dating for…um…some time, so you can imagine."

I never would've thought a man like him would be so affected by his feelings. I wouldn't imagine he even has feelings. Wrong of me, maybe, but I can't help it. He just comes across that way. "I'm sorry. That really sucks. I can only imagine."

"Have you ever had the privilege of watching an ex you haven't yet gotten over get married?"

"No. No, I can't say that I have."

He nods slowly. "You're right, then. You can only imagine."

I can't help but toy with the bedspread a little as I try making heads or tails of where this is going. Am I his therapist now? "So, you need somebody to accompany you to this wedding."

"Correct."

"No offense intended, but don't you have female friends?"

His smile is slow. "No. I can honestly say there are no female friends in my life."

"Because why would a man want to be friends with a woman?" I can't help but roll my eyes even though he's in the power position right now. I've never been a fan of men who don't understand that women are more than pleasure bots, or whatever they think we are.

"I'm not highly skilled in male-female relationships, and I don't do things I'm not good at."

I want to ask how he expects to ever get good at it then, but something tells me that would be completely pointless.

"And any female acquaintances may…um…misconstrue an offer such as this. Besides, my ex has a nose for such things. A brand new face would be best."

I get what he's saying and can almost imagine some of his acquaintances. Bubble-breasted bimbo gold diggers who would expect more than a trip to Vegas with a man as good-looking and rich as him. Because he's obviously loaded. His Rolex could pay my rent for years, and I've seen the other three watches in a case on his dresser. "What are you asking? That I attend this wedding as your plus one?" Oh, my God, can I really do something like this? I don't know this guy. He could be anybody. And he's so darn pushy. Bossy. I can't imagine we'd get along well, as that sort of attitude always rubs me up the wrong way.

He smiles, showing off a perfect row of straight, perfectly pearly teeth. He really is extremely, extremely hot.

I'm just about ready to faint from sexiness overload, when his grin gets wider, almost wolfish.

"I'll need a little more than that in return, Dani."

I take a deep gasping breath and stand. "What do you mean?"

"I'll need you to act as my fiancée and pretend you're in love with me."

CHAPTER 9

Dani

Now I'm sure I'm going to faint, so it's a good thing the bed is just behind my legs. I sink down, hard. This impossibly handsome billionaire wants to take me with him to Vegas! "You want me to pretend we're engaged—and in love." It isn't a question. I just need to say it out loud to be sure I'm not imagining things.

"That's right."

I gaze at him with wide eyes. "Why? Why me? A complete stranger?"

He leans forward again, and this time I catch a whiff of his cologne. That musky, spicy, intoxicating scent makes my head spin worse than it already is. Not fair. He's just so damn hot. I need to get my brain functioning properly because things just got real.

"For one thing, you're a beautiful woman."

I blush and turn my face slightly away.

"You must know it's true, so don't put on the shy act. Beautiful women know on some level how beautiful they are." He pauses, his eyes shining. "Though, I must admit, you've probably looked better than you do at the moment."

I run a self-conscious hand over my sleep-mussed hair. "Thanks. I got this way after scouring your apartment."

"And the effort is appreciated." He sits back, grinning wickedly. "Another reason: you're honest. Honesty goes a long way in my book. The fact that you made the effort to do the job correctly rather than balling up another set of sheets from the closet and throwing them into the laundry chute says a lot about your character. I appreciate that. I'll need a woman with character if we're going to pull this off."

"A woman with character who will lie for you." I really don't know why I'm smirking.

"A woman with character who I can trust not to try to take advantage of me."

"What does that mean? How would I even go about doing that?"

He pauses, blue eyes a little wider, as though he's marveling at me. "You honestly have no idea. I'm liking you more and more with each passing moment, Dani."

"I don't even know your name."

"Brock," it rolls off his tongue like something dark, sensual and borderline dangerous.

"Well, Brock, I don't know how I feel about this offer."

"I appreciate your honesty." He tents his fingers under his chin again, as he was doing when I woke up and found him watching me sleep—how creepy is that?—and says, "I enjoy negotiating and I'm prepared to do just that. Let me warn you however, that I've been known to drive a hard bargain."

Terrific. I have to get myself in order and stop wondering what he'd look like without his shirt on. My heart's beating so fast, I'm afraid I might be sick. I need to outfox him, somehow. My competitive nature won't allow me to give in. "All right." I swallow hard. "I assume you'd want us to share a room when we're there."

"A suite," he corrects.

"Fine. A suite." That makes things a bit better, or does it? "I would appreciate there being an arrangement in place for us to sleep separately."

"Naturally."

That was easy. Maybe too easy. "I would expect to sleep in the bed, of course."

He chuckles. "We both will. It'll be a two-bedroom affair."

My mouth goes dry at his choice of words. I lick my lips. "Uh...I would probably need something nice enough to wear to a wedding," I admit, the old shame comes flooding back as I look down at my hands. His cleaning woman, admitting she doesn't have nice clothes. Because she's never had nice clothes. She may no longer rely on Goodwill, but her wardrobe would never fly in Brock's circle. I can't help but laugh softly at myself. "Funny how stupid little things can bring up old baggage. I'm not exactly proud to admit I don't have a nice dress."

"Baggage is tricky," he agrees, but there's a new softness in his voice which surprises me.

My head snaps up. I look up at him defiantly. I don't want him pitying me, or anything. I've worked hard for everything I've got and I'm not ashamed of anything I've done.

He smiles. "No worries. I wasn't intending to let you go to the wedding with me before purchasing a suitable wardrobe for you."

A wardrobe? "What's that, now?"

"This is a weekend-long agreement. You would need more than just a dress for the wedding. I planned to purchase clothing which pleases me."

I raise an eyebrow. "Why should it please you?"

He shrugs. "I'm the one buying it."

I fold my arms in front of me. "I'm the one wearing it."

"You don't have to wear it." His eyes flicker over my body.

Now, a shiver runs through me. "Yeah, and I don't have to go with you."

He looks me in the eye at this challenge and we stare at each other for a long, silent moment. What's going on in his head? I wish I knew, though I'm not even certain I'd be comfortable with the answer.

He clears his throat. "Wearing clothing that I find attractive is hardly a wise sticking point, Dani," he warns. "I promise I have excellent taste, and since I will have no use for them, they would be a gift to you. You could keep them. I would like you to."

"So long as they're comfortable and I like them too. I'm not spending the weekend walking around looking like a fetish porn model, or something."

It's his turn to raise an eyebrow. "Hmm. Now there's an idea."

I frown. "I mean it."

He waves his hand. "Cool your jets. You're quite safe. My proclivities don't run in that direction." There go his eyes again, straying further south. "Though I could be persuaded to change my mind."

"Eyes up here, please." I point to my own eyes.

He obeys with a cheeky, little-boy-caught-being-naughty smile.

I know he should irritate me to the point of slapping him and storming out, but I just can't seem to muster up the indignation. Maybe because he's so darn charming. Maybe because he seems like a fairly honorable person. Or maybe the truth, because he's so frigging sexy that I want him to flirt and talk dirty to me.

"Anything else you're concerned about?" he asks.

"Public displays of affection."

His eyes glitter suddenly. "Personally, I believe in discretion, tact. The sight of couples slobbering all over each other in public is unnecessary. Public sex, I wouldn't rule out—but somewhere discreet."

"I'll keep that in mind," I mutter, shaking my head at him. He's a real piece of work. I can't make sense of him.

"However, we'll have to play it by ear. While I've never forced myself on a woman and don't intend on starting with you, some intimacy will be expected of a newly engaged couple."

"What sort of intimacy?"

"Some hand holding."

I nod.

"A quick kiss."

I take a deep breath and nod.

"An arm around the waist—perhaps a little lower than the waist…"

"Watch it," I warn.

"We have to be convincing, don't we?" And now he's all innocence. He's having fun with me.

CHAPTER 10

Dani

W hat am I getting myself into? I can't believe I'm actually considering this. "You will pay for the airfare?"

"We'll be taking my private jet."

God, I must sound so hopelessly backward. "Of course, I should've known."

"Money is a problem for you, isn't it?" His eyes have that intensity to them again.

"A rude question."

"Which means the answer is yes." He sighs, tapping his fingers together. "I wasn't going to bring up this part of the bargain so early, but I'm willing to do so if it helps you make your decision."

"And what would that be?"

"The fact that I'm willing to pay two hundred and fifty thousand dollars for the pleasure of your company."

My jaw drops. It literally drops. He said it like it was nothing. I stare at him, speechless. A quarter of a million dollars! What I couldn't do with that kind of money. It's enough to make my head spin. Actually, I can't even do the math right now because my brain is somewhere far away, floating along in the ether. I'm pretty sure it might even be lost forever.

He waves his hand in front of my face. "Did I lose you?"

"I-I mean—are you serious?"

"I don't play games."

I shake my head, blinking rapidly in the struggle to get control of myself. At least five years. If I keep living on the cheap, as I do now, I could support myself for five years on that much money. At least.

Four years, if I decide to take a vacation or two.

Wow, I could go to school full-time and stop working.

I could live like a girl my age wants to live.

I'd have time for friends again, and for fun.

I'd be able to live my life instead of falling asleep over my books every night and cleaning up after rich slobs everyday.

"I wish I knew what to say..." I whisper, still trying to come up with something, before reality hits, and my eyes narrow into dangerous slits. "Hold on. You want me to believe that all I have to do is go away with you for a weekend, on your private jet, and hang out in Vegas with the two of us sleeping separately? For that much money? You really want me to believe that?"

"I do." He raises one hand, a finger extended straight up. "However, there's one more catch."

"I knew it. I knew this was too good to be true." And I'm about ten seconds from running out the door.

"You have to move in here with me until we leave for the wedding, which is this weekend."

"Oh, come on. And I suppose we're just going to accidentally bump into each other on the way to or from the shower and oops, your towel's going to fall off and whoops, we just fall onto the bed together—"

"Dani."

The word is like a whip cutting through the air. It stuns me into silence.

He stares at me, his eyes so brilliantly blue, it is like a photograph of the ocean around one of those tropical paradises in the magazines on the coffee tables of the houses I clean. "I've already told you, I don't force myself on women and I do not play games. I've already stated the obvious, that you're beautiful, and I'll admit to allowing myself the pleasure of admiring your body. This isn't some elaborate ruse to lure you into my bed. I don't need a random woman to fuck. And even if I did, I wouldn't pay for it and certainly not that much money."

I'm shaking. There's another side to him, one much more in keeping with how demanding he is when it comes to the condition of his apartment. A coiled power, just under the surface. He keeps it under control. But just barely.

"I'm still in love with my ex-girlfriend." Suddenly, his voice sounds strained.

My heart's racing faster than an express train. I actually feel a little woozy. "Why—why do you want me to move in here, then? What for?"

"To make this as believable as possible. I don't go into anything without preparing first, and I want to prepare the both of us so we'll make a convincing couple." His eyes narrow, just enough to make me shiver a little. "And I want to be sure you're safe. New York isn't safe."

My eyes widen with shock. No one has ever cared enough to check whether I'm safe. I've watched my own back for as long as I can remember. "That's ridiculous. You don't have the first idea about my life or how I live it."

"That's irrelevant. I have OCD tendencies. When you're here with me, living under my roof, I'll know for certain." He grins. "Would you rather I call you every ten minutes to be sure?"

I accept the olive branch and grin back. "That isn't the least bit troublesome, or insane," I quip drily.

"Would you?" he challenges.

I chew at my bottom lip. "No. I wouldn't rather you call me every ten minutes. I wouldn't even give you my number."

"Do you want to see how quickly I can find it?"

"No. Thanks very much."

He looks about as satisfied as the cat that ate the cream— another of my foster mother's favorite sayings. He knows he has me where he wants me, that's why.

I shift my weight from one foot to the other. "I could take one of the other rooms?"

"Naturally."

"And it would only be until the weekend, when we would go to Las Vegas? And I would move home after that?"

"Of course."

Somehow, that didn't come out as sure and strong as the first agreement. I wonder why not. What does he think? That I'll let him control my movements even when this is over? He's got another think coming—but hey, he wants to get to know me, doesn't he? That's why I'm moving in with him. Well, he'll get to know me, all right. "I'm pretty sure I'll end up regretting this," I whisper.

"I'm certain you won't. I'll make sure you don't."

"I have to wonder what you mean by that."

"You'll have to wait and see." He stands, towering over me.

Boy, he's tall. This is the first time I'm seeing his full height. When I stand too, he dwarfs me. I'm around five-five, so he has to be almost a foot taller. Whew. "Am I honestly accepting this crazy idea?"

Brock smiles, his eyes are warm and sparkling for the first time since I woke up. "If you're half as smart as you seem, you are. This is the sort of arrangement any girl would kill to be a part of."

"Because you're so wonderful?" I challenge.

"Because you need the money. And I have more than I know what to do with. In fact, this is likely the first time in a very,

very long time that I've ever been truly satisfied with the result of spending it." He extends a hand to seal our deal.

I can't believe I'm about to do this. I absolutely *cannot* believe it's happening. Like something out of a dream, or a fantasy story. Not my life, certainly. And yet, it's his hand swallowing up mine in a strong grip. It's his firm handshake. It's him, I'm swaying closer to, almost touching my body to his because he's so overwhelming, I can barely stand up straight.

And he knows it, the scoundrel.

CHAPTER 11

Dani

My hands are shaking as I pull out my cell to call the only person who I think might come close to understanding what I just went through. Not that Penelope has ever been propositioned the way I've just been. But she gets me. She's been in my shoes. We share a history, even if we've only known each other for a few years.

"Penn. Oh, my God." I can barely get the words out, I'm breathing so heavy.

"What's wrong? What happened? Are you all right?" Her normally smooth, mellow voice is shot through with fear.

"I'm sorry. I didn't mean to freak you out. I just—I can't believe what just happened. I need a second to catch my breath."

"But you're all right?"

"I'm all right." I think. I hope.

"So what happened?"

"I think I just did something really stupid. Or really amazing. Or both." I'm still sitting on one of the chairs in the restrooms on the ground floor of his building. I don't trust myself to go out onto the street. My head is still spinning and I'd probably walk into traffic and get killed.

"I swear, girl, if you don't tell me what it is, I'm going to scream!"

"Sorry, sorry." I take a deep breath. "I texted you earlier and told you about the job Helen sent me on today."

"Yeah, you did. How much will you end up getting for it?"

"Oh, I don't even know. Whatever it comes to after Helen's cut and taxes." Funny, how I've stopped thinking about that already.

"What will you do with the money?" She cackles in glee at the idea of such a huge sum.

Boy, do I have news for her.

"That's not the news, though. Penn. This is the news." I pause to take a deep breath. "The guy who I was cleaning for wants me to go to Vegas with him this weekend and pretend to be his fiancée at his ex's wedding."

Silence. For a long time. "What?" she finally gasps.

"You heard me."

"To Las Vegas? For the weekend?"

"Yes."

"He's footing the bill?" Amazing how we think along the same lines. An after-effect of the way we both grew up. We might have been thousands of miles apart at the time, but we know what the other one went through.

"Oh, he's more than footing the bill. He's buying me clothes to wear there, and we're taking his private jet, and staying in a suite in a fancy hotel."

"Uh, Dani…"

"I know, I know. It all sounds too goddamned good to be true."

"He's not some pervert sicko, is he?"

"I don't think so. I sure hope not."

"I guess you have to sleep with him, huh?"

"No."

"No?" she echoes in shock.

"He told me he didn't want that from me. He's still in love with his ex. I guess it's an ego thing for him. He wants to show that he is all right without her or something."

"What's he like?"

I blow out a deep, heavy breath. "Oh, Penn. He's gorgeous. I mean drop-dead gorgeous. Almost a foot taller than me, dark hair, the bluest eyes you ever saw…" I realize I'm getting a little giddy. I sound like I have a crush, like a teenager with a crush on the captain of the football team.

"I hate you so much right now!" she squeals.

"Then, wait until I tell you the best part."

"You haven't yet?"

"Nope. He's giving me two hundred and fifty thousand dollars for doing this."

Silence. Longer, this time. "Oh, my giddy aunt! That's—that's a *lot* of money. Hang on…did you get the money yet? Do you even have proof that it exists?"

"He's rich as sin, Penn."

"That doesn't matter. Ever hear about debt, dear? He could be in it up to his eyeballs, for all you know. I would definitely get a look at his bank statements before I agreed."

"It's too late," I whisper with my eyes squeezed shut.

"You already said you would!"

"I did. It's nuts, right? I'm insane. I did something completely insane and it's so unlike me, I don't even know what to think." I hold my head in my free hand, rubbing my forehead as it all comes crashing down. Penn is right. It's too good to be true. *Wake up, Dani. This is the real world. Who pays someone two hundred and fifty thousand dollars just to pretend to be their fiancée for a weekend?* There has to be more to this. I exhale slowly, the rush of excitement dying out. Making me suddenly feel sad and depressed. Of course, things like this never happen to me. I feel my body slide down the wall of the restroom and I end up squatting on the floor.

"I don't have to go back to him," I say quietly. "I can just call it quits and move on and I don't have to go through with it."

"Now wait a minute. Wait just one minute. I never said that, girlfriend."

"Then you're sending pretty mixed signals, Penn."

"I just think you should exercise caution, is all. Find out if the money even exists, but you know. Hell, Dani, even if it doesn't, you're getting a fabulous Vegas weekend out of it. With a gorgeous man. And if he wants sex. Go for it. How often do you get a new wardrobe bought for you and whisked off to Vegas for the weekend by a billionaire? Never is the short answer."

I giggle.

"I hate you sometimes," she grumbles.

"If you think it, you mean it…"

We both laugh.

"So you don't think this is wrong?" I ask again.

"You know what's more important? How you feel about it. The fact that you even have to ask whether I think it's wrong, tells me you have misgivings."

"A Psych major, through and through," I mutter.

"I mean it. You have to be okay with it personally."

I stand up and square my shoulders. "I believe him when he says he won't do anything wrong, and I've already gotten his word on that. Believe me."

"I believe you did. You're not a dummy. Although, if he's that hot, don't you think you should be jumping his bones?"

"I don't want to think about it like that. I don't like the idea of it. He said he doesn't play games and has no intention of luring me into his bed. He only wants me to pretend to be his fiancée."

"So you'll have to pretend to be crazy about him."

"I've gotta admit, I don't think I'll have to try too hard," I whisper, since I don't even know how I feel about this next little admission. "He's really something."

"You already said he was a dream. You don't have to rub it in."

"I don't mean that—not just that, anyway. I don't know what it is. He's sexy and alluring and smart. He appreciates honesty and character, and we both know how sexy that is."

"And how unbelievably rare," she snorts.

"I think, no…I know, if we ran in the same circles, I would like him as a friend. Yeah, he's weird in some ways. Even obsessive when it comes to having things done a certain way. It took all day to get his place cleaned. He's tough too, in a strong, silent way. I get the feeling that whatever he does, he's a big deal."

"With all that money, I bet he is."

"You know money doesn't mean a person is a big deal. He could've inherited it, or just got lucky with a windfall, but I don't think so. He said he likes to negotiate, and was just away on a business trip. I think he's a big deal for sure. He's definitely used to having his own way."

"Oh. You'll go together like oil and water."

"We already do." I snicker. "We've already shared a few choice words. I don't take well to being ordered around, and told him so."

"Good!"

"That being said, I'm moving into his apartment for the rest of the week."

"What? No. Way."

"It's just so we can get to know each other better. I mean, it's Monday night. It's not like I'll be there forever. We'll fly out Friday morning. A few days, staying in one of the guest rooms. Hey, it'll be like a real vacation. I haven't had one of those in…ever."

"But. Do you have to?"

"It's one of his conditions and yes, I admit that it gave me pause at first. But it's only a few days. And I do need to get to know him if I'm going to be convincing."

"That's true. I guess it's like that movie Green Card where they learn each other's ways and habits, so they don't trip up in front of the immigration officers," she says dreamily.

"I do want to do a good job. I don't want to let him down. I'll do everything in my power to make his ex, regret leaving him."

"You work so hard at everything you ever try, I already feel sorry for her."

"I do go the extra mile, don't I?" I tell her about the sheets.

She laughs uproariously. "That is so typical of you! So he appreciated that, huh?"

"He did."

"I always knew that being such an insufferable perfectionist with a nonstop work ethic would pay off one day. Good for you."

"Insufferable." I chuckle. "Good to know how you really feel about me."

RIVER LAURENT

"You know what I mean. You're just too perfect."

I catch the sight of my own brown eyes in the mirror. "Yeah. Perfect." I'm anything but, and she knows it, but I get her point. I am a stickler for perfection and order. Like him.

"And now, a perfect man noticed your perfection! You deserve this!"

"I'm hardly perfect, but thanks, I think?"

"Girl, he's the golden goose that laid the golden egg."

"Is that what they're calling it these days?" I laugh. "I'm standing in the restroom of his building shaking in my shoes."

"Why?"

"Because I did the math and it's going to mean I can quit my stupid job and focus on wrapping up school. I need this money more than I even want to admit to myself and I think I'm just scared that it's too good to be true."

"Sometimes good things happen to good people, Dani. It's about time you had a break. It's not the money. It's what the money represents. Your freedom. I couldn't be happier for you."

CHAPTER 12

Dani

Suddenly, I have memory flash. I'm back in the small house I lived in with my parents. The Child Protection Officers are there. They're telling my mother and father that the others kids have reported me for selling my body in school the day before. I can see my mother's face vividly. It is white with horror. I try to tell them that I only wanted to help, but my father won't even look at me. And my mother is so ashamed she hangs her head.

I take a deep breath. Wow, that was so long ago and yet it has remained so fresh in my memory banks. "And it doesn't make me a whore? Taking all that money?" I ask slowly.

"What? You're being paid to act like his fiancée. If you then chose to screw him because you want him like mad, that's your fucking business. Your life. You hear me? Just be smart about this." She pauses. "But I know you wouldn't, because that's not your style. And I know something else, too."

"What?"

"You won't let yourself have any fun."

"You don't know that!"

"Sure, I don't." She laughs. "You won't, because you don't know how to."

Ouch. That one hits a little closer to home than I like, because she's right. I've never been able to devote any time to fun. I've never had a vacation. No Spring Breaks for me, no trips to Europe, or Mexico as a graduation present. I've been working since I was thirteen, as soon as I could get papers stating I was eligible. I was the Girl Without Parents, the Foster Kid, the one who never belonged. Penelope is my only true friend, plus a few casual acquaintances I sometimes chat with before, or after class. But most of my classes are online, so I'm fairly insulated from the world.

"Is that weird? That I don't know how to have fun?"

"No. Not weird. But something you should work on. This is your chance. Live it up a little! Go shopping, hit the slots, or the poker tables, drink all you want, have a ball. He's paying for it."

"That's true. I guess, I could. He doesn't seem like the type who would begrudge me a bit of fun. I'll find out more about him before we go and we'll see."

She let out a sound between a growl and a groan. "Honey, you are gorgeous. You're smart and sweet and you've got a kickin' bod. He wants you with him because you'll make him look good in front of his ex. He might think he's in control of the situation, but you are. Remember that when you want to enjoy yourself, and you'll find a way to convince him."

Her knowing laugh makes me laugh, but it also makes me blush and bite down hard on my bottom lip. I can't stop thinking about his eyes, and his smile and oh, God, his body under that expensive suit of his.

And the way he looked at me. The way his eyes trailed over my body whenever he got the chance. He said I was beautiful. I don't think he was lying about that. He's attracted to me. Admitting it to myself makes my heart race all over again.

Him. Attracted to me. Whoa!

"This still feels so crazy," I whisper.

"Probably because it is." She chuckles. "But that doesn't mean it isn't amazing. Because it's definitely that. Just promise you're gonna keep me updated all the time. Okay? I mean, even if you have to check in while you're staying with him. I don't want my girl staying with a guy who's gonna wear her skin."

"You always say the sweetest things."

"Also update me if he wants to turn the twosome action into a ménage scenario."

"Eww," I scream.

We're both giggling as we get off the phone. As always, a talk with Penn makes me feel better. I can do this, and I'll have a great time while I'm at it.

And when it's all over, I'll have the kind of bank account that

I could only dream of until now. I can't help but plan for the future as I stroll out of the restroom.

As I get to the door, a man in uniform runs up to me. "Dani Saber," he asks.

"Yes."

"Let me show you to your ride."

For a second I can only blink, then I follow him out to the street. A gleaming limo is idling on the street waiting for me. He opens the back door and I slip inside the perfumed interior.

The driver opens the glass partition and smiles. "Good evening, Miss Saber. My name is Tom. Where can I drop you off?"

I give him my Red Bank address.

He nods and closes the partition.

The car begins its smooth journey. *Wow, this is the life.*

When a text buzzes on my phone, my smile fades.

BROCK: Why did it take you so long to get to the lobby? Is everything all right?

What the hell? Is he monitoring me? I decide to ask him as much. *Are you some sort of stalker now?*

BROCK: No, but I had my driver parked illegally. You spent an extra fifteen minutes in there. I was about to go down and make sure you were all right.

Wow. He's intense. *Uh, thanks. Everything is fine. I made a phone call from the Ladies.*

BROCK: *From now on, please let me know when you plan on doing something like that.*

I can't stand another minute of this crap. I call him up instead of wearing out my thumbs texting everything that's on my mind. "What's with this caveman macho act? That sort of thing went out of style a long time ago."

"Hello to you, too, Dani."

"I mean it," I snarl. "I don't need to tell you when I'm making a phone call, Brock. In case you forgot, we only met this evening. And while it's true that you have employed me to go to this wedding as your fiancée, it doesn't give you the right to dictate what I do." Penn would be so proud of me right now. I'm sort of proud of myself, in fact.

"I won't apologize for being concerned about your well-being, now that we have an arrangement in place."

"Having an arrangement in place doesn't mean you own me."

"No, but it means I'm investing money in you, and I don't want to lose on this investment."

I blink. "I'm an investment?"

"You're an investment of money—and time, which I value above all else."

"You don't have to invest a thing in me, Mr. Brock Whatever Your Last Name Is. I didn't ask you to bestow this great honor on me, and I don't want you to."

"Do you really mean that?"

"What do you think?"

For a few seconds, all I hear is the sound of his breathing. I

73

wonder what's going through his head. He can't like being told off like this, but he had it coming to him.

"Fair enough. If this is all too much for you, you're free to do as you choose. If you decide not to take me up on my offer, it was nice knowing you. Though I plan on docking a percentage of your pay for skipping on my bedroom."

Just like that, the call is over and I'm right back where I started from. My foster mother always did warn me that my mouth would get me into trouble. I sit back, utterly dejected. Well, it was nice while it lasted, the idea of all that money. All that freedom.

Buzz, buzz.

My eyes snap down to my phone.

BROCK: *In case you're still in, I'll have a car pick you up at nine tomorrow.*

Damn him. I manage to wait twenty minutes before replying. *Okay. I'll be ready.*

CHAPTER 13

Dani

He's true to his word. The car is waiting outside my building at eight-forty-five the next morning.

I wish I had chosen a better time for him to arrive. Pre-dawn, maybe. I could've made the sacrifice if it meant avoiding the nosy gazes of my neighbors as they left for work, or came back from dropping their kids off at school. Not that Red Bank is a dump. Well, I guess, it is compared to Brock's penthouse, obviously, but not in general. Even so, nobody expects to see a limousine parked at the curb of a converted three-story house with a chain-link fence separating the side yard from the sidewalk.

There are a few whistles in the air as I hurry out to the porch, struggling to get my wheeled luggage down the uneven, wood planked steps.

Tom gets out, wearing a dark blue suit and hurries over to me. "Let me help you with that, Miss Saber."

"Oh. Thank you." Actually, I nearly told him I can manage, but I remember just in time that I'd better get used to treatment like this if I expect to be believable as the fiancée of a man like Brock. He wouldn't pick just anybody off the street. His girl would have to be sophisticated, sharp, worldly.

Well, I'm none of those things. I'm barely removed from the days of wearing ill-fitting, grease-stinking clothes from the Goodwill. There are certain formative experiences which never wash away. That's one of them. I carry it around with me like a badge, but not of honor. Of shame, more like. I still get the feeling sometimes that people are watching me, judging me. The way they're watching as I climb into the back seat of the limo. But I can pretend. And I can pretend good.

Now that I'm on the other side of the tinted glass, I turn to look at my neighbors.

Mrs. Morgan is smoking one of her day's many cigarettes. The old mason jar which she converted to an ashtray sits on the wooden railing, waiting to be crammed with hundreds of butts. She ashes over the side, onto the plastic flowers. The only things she can manage to keep alive.

Her porch adjoins Mrs. Weaver's, and the two of them are muttering to each other over the bannister which separates them as Mrs. Morgan gestures to Brock's car with her cigarette.

They just happen to be the only two outside at the moment. There are others watching from inside their homes, pulling back faded curtains to get a look at what that strange, reclusive, dark-haired girl is up to. I can just imagine what they're thinking and saying in their thick North Jersey accents.

Is she some sorta big shot or somethin'?

Who does she think she is?

Who's she friends with?

Must be nice...

"Are you ready, Miss Saber?"

I realize the driver is speaking to me and smile gratefully. "Absolutely. Thank you."

He grins at me and at that moment I decide to forget my gossiping neighbors. They're nothing. They can only make me feel as small as I allow them to make me feel. One of the many self-help mantras I've mastered over the years of trying to get past my troubled youth.

It comes back to me in moments like this. Even sitting in this sleek, ultra-comfortable car with its buttery leather and a minibar inside. I can't help but go right back to being that poor little girl everyone laughed at again. I remind myself that she's in the past. Just a page in my history, and I'm stronger as a result of what she had to go through. Even so, I hate it when people stare at me.

Penelope's advice rings in my head. *Have fun.*

She's so right. When will I ever have the chance to do something like this again? I'm going to live the life of a glamorous, wealthy woman, and pretend to be the fiancée of a gorgeous billionaire. I don't know who his ex is, but holy cow, she must be something else not to keep him. I'm going to make the most of it, and that means no more negativity. Brock won't want to hear about it, and he's the one paying me to pretend with him. I'm going to turn this experience into the best vacation ever.

First though, there's something I just have to know. "Excuse me?" I call out to the driver.

"Yes, Miss?"

"Oh, you can call me Dani." I scoot forward until I'm seated just behind him, since I can't imagine shouting throughout the ride even if it's a short one. "I have a crazy question for you."

"What can I help you with?" He's middle-aged, maybe late forties, with kind eyes.

I feel like I can trust him. "How long have you been driving for Brock?"

"Mr. Garret?"

Oh, right. His last name. I didn't think to ask for it. I have to be smarter.

"I suppose it's been nearly three years now."

"Have you picked up a lot of different girls in this car?"

I see him blanche in the rearview mirror.

"Don't worry, I won't tell your boss. We're not romantically involved or anything like that. I don't even care outside of wondering where I fit in here. Does he do this sort of thing often?"

"Send me out to Red Bank to pick up a charming young woman?"

I roll my eyes, but can't help giggling.

"No. He does not."

"You mean that? Like I said, I won't rat you out or anything like that. I just want to know what I'm dealing with."

"Scout's honor." He grimaces a little, like he doesn't know whether or not he should share the next bit of info.

"Go on," I encourage.

"It's not as though he's a saint. He has his girlfriends, of course, but they're nothing like you. They're usually a bit... uppity, if you know what I mean." He lifts his nose to demonstrate.

I laugh.

"And he's certainly never invited a young lady to move in with him for any length of time." He meets my eyes in the rear view. "You have a suitcase. It doesn't take a genius to put two and two together."

My cheeks go red. "It's not like—"

"It doesn't make a bit of difference to me," he says with a shrug. "You're pleasant company."

"Thank you, Tom. For the record, Mr. Garret is paying me to stay with him and oh, God—that didn't come out the way I meant it to." I bury my red-hot face in my hands.

He chuckles. "Please, don't worry. You won't find any judgment from this area of the car. And I can tell you're not that sort of girl. For one—and I don't mean this in a negative way, not whatsoever—the sorts of girls who charge for their time don't normally live in such a modest area."

I smile. "That's a very gentle way of pointing out how poor I am."

"I don't mean any insult by it."

"And I didn't take it as an insult. I understand what you're trying to say."

He grins at me.

CHAPTER 14

Dani

I decide to let him get back to driving. I know I should be having fun with this situation, but it seems unlikely considering the fluttery feeling in my stomach whenever I remember the way Brock looked at me. Also, there's still a lot of pressure on my shoulders.

I don't want to trip up in Vegas, and make a fool of both of us. I want to be convincing. I have to make his ex believe that we are madly in love, even if I'm not the usual type of girl he goes out with.

A thought occurs to me. What happens if he decides at the end of the weekend that I didn't do a job worthy of the huge amount he's offered me? He seems to be genuine, but I really should get something in writing. I wish I knew a lawyer. He seems smart enough to know how to create loopholes...and he did say he is a tough negotiator, but he didn't negotiate hard with me at all.

This part baffles me most of all.

Is my company really worth that amount of money? He doesn't even know me, but he's willing to offer more money than I could hope to make in seven or eight years. How could he possibly thinks he's getting the better end of the deal?

This girl must have really hurt him if he's this desperate to prove to her he is over her. If she turned him down, she must be one of those uppity girls. I can't understand how he thinks a girl like me will make a woman like her jealous.

Me? I look down at my good outfit—skinny jeans, knee-high riding boots, a thigh-length blue cardigan. What's so special about me? My hair is thick and pretty enough, I guess, but brown. Plain brown, just like my eyes. And I'm too curvy. I'd give just about anything to be able to wear a button-down blouse without worrying about a button popping off and taking out somebody's eye. Average height, average looks. Average just about everything.

Not like him. He's special. Which tells me she must be *very* special, whoever she is. Maybe he'll tell me, or better still, I'll snoop around online and find out for myself. I need to know who I'm up against. Just the thought of being up against anybody—especially a girl who made a deep enough impression on him to warrant the sort of scheme I'm getting myself wrapped up in—makes my heart race a little.

As long as he puts things in writing, that is.

"What took you so long?"

The sound of his voice, not to mention the irritation in it, makes my head jerk up.

He's waiting on the second floor, looking over the living room with his hands palm-down on the banister. He's just as sexy in a black sweater and jeans as he is in a suit. The way the cashmere—and I'm betting its cashmere—wraps itself around his thick arms is darn near miraculous.

But he's so brusque, the part of me that's not drooling get pissed off. Still, what did I expect? Roses and a seat by the fire? This is a business arrangement. I close the door slowly. "It took as long as it took to get here," I explain with a shrug. "Have you ever been to Red Bank?"

A muscle jumps in his clenched jaw. He looks mad at something. "No. It's not exactly a place I've had on my bucket list."

"I don't think it's on anybody's bucket list."

His expression softens. "I didn't mean it like that. I was concerned."

"Why?" I ask curiously. Either he's the most possessive man in the world, or there's a reason for him to be so anxiously over-the-top all the time. I realize I'm trying to analyze him like a case study out of one of my textbooks and chide myself. I'm doing this for the money. After the weekend, I'll never see him again.

His hands tighten on the banister. "Maybe I was just worried you wouldn't keep to your end of the bargain."

"If this is going to work you need to cut down on the caffeine and chill. I always keep my word." I stare into his watching blue eyes. "Always."

He smiles slowly. "Thank you."

When I start wheeling my suitcase toward the stairs, he jogs down to meet me. "Here. I'll take care of that for you." He lifts it with ease.

I follow him up to one of the guest rooms, striving not to trip over my feet as I stare at his firm butt. Holy moly, what a view.

"Why did you pack so much?" he asks, putting the suitcase on the bed. "I told you I'd buy everything you need for the weekend."

"That's very generous of you, but maybe too generous, because it made me feel bad. I brought a few things I thought might be worthwhile—"

He waves his hands almost like he's shooing away a fly or a bee. "No, no. I want to start you fresh. In fact, you have an appointment with Veronica at Bergdorf in twenty minutes."

My head starts spinning. "You set up an appointment for me at Bergdorf?" I gasp.

"Yes, I have an account there. Veronica is my personal shopper. She has an excellent eye. I've already sent her the rundown of what you'll require. She only needs to see you, take a few measurements, and fit you up with the necessary clothes."

"You—uh—don't want to see these things before you pay for them?" I must look completely confused. I certainly feel that way.

He shakes his head. "No. I trust her." Then he moves forward and ushers me from the room and down the stairs with a firm but gentle hand on the small of my back.

The pressure is light, but I'm keenly aware of his touch.

In a kind of daze, I watch his large hand snake past me and hit the button on the elevator panel. I haven't had the chance to ask him about putting our agreement in writing yet, but I don't even know how to broach the subject. I stand there staring at the closed elevator doors.

"Have fun," he says cheerfully when the doors open. "Enjoy having somebody take care of you for once."

It's like he already knows me. How can he make a statement like that and sound so sure of himself, and be so right? "It's just that I thought you would be coming with me," I admit. Truth is I'm intimidated by the thought of going on my own.

He grins wolfishly. "I have work to do. Otherwise, I would."

I step onto the elevator and stop just short of asking why I didn't go straight to the store instead of stopping at the penthouse. I don't exactly love the sensation of being shuffled back and forth. Only when the doors are starting to slide shut between us do I get up the nerve to ask, "Should I call if the shopping runs a little long?"

His eyes snap blue fire, but a ghost of a smile tugs at the corners of his mouth. "No."

Then the doors shut on him.

CHAPTER 15

Dani

"You look gorgeous," Veronica purrs, walking around me in a slow circle as she taps impeccably manicured, deep red nails against her chin. "Absolutely stunning."

"Are you sure about that?" I wish I was. I don't feel stunning at all. If anything, I feel downright exposed. I didn't know until this very minute that it was possible for a person to feel exposed when so much of their body was covered, but here I am. Sleek, black, with a high collar which fastens around my neck. It's cut down to the middle of my back, sleeveless, and hits just above my knee. Completely respectable. Classy. Wildly expensive. And unnerving.

"Don't you like it?" The strident, confident, no-nonsense saleswoman peers at me in the mirror from over my shoulder.

I slide my hands over my stomach and around to my hips, gliding over the lush fabric. It's like looking at a stranger, but I can feel my body, and my body can feel my hands on it. So it must be me. Just a version of me I've never seen before. One I didn't know existed up until now.

And this is just one dress! There are other dresses for both night and day, skirts, shoes and even pajamas and underwear. Veronica seems to know my body better than just about anybody ever has except for maybe my jerk of an ex-boyfriend.

I turn to check out my profile. "It's not that I don't like it. It's absolutely gorgeous, but I'm not sure it is me."

"Not you? Honey, this dress was made for you."

I frown. I've just never dressed like this. I really hope I can carry this glamorous act off successfully.

Suddenly, she places her hands on my shoulders and turns me to face her. She's old enough to be my mother, I guess, and that combined with the few inches she has on me makes me feel like a little girl. "Do you know what I see in front of me?" she asks.

I shake my head.

"I see a beautiful girl who caught the eye of—between you and me—the sexiest man to walk the streets of Manhattan." There's a naughty twinkle in her eyes.

A giggle erupts from me, and I clamp a hand over my mouth. She seems so worldly and sophisticated, I didn't expect her to be so blunt.

She winks like we're old friends. After the way she's

measured me and dressed me today, we practically are. "I say, enjoy yourself. Trust me, his eyes will fall out of his head when he sees you in any of the dresses I've picked out for you, but especially this one."

"As much as I'd hate for him to lose his eyes…"

We share a laugh and suddenly, I feel much better.

Once I'm finished dressing in my own clothes, which suddenly looks cheap and shabby, I step out of the dressing room to find her going over the list Brock dictated.

"All right. It looks like this is all of it," she says to her assistant, a meek and mousy girl who flashes a shy smile at me.

There's an entire rack of new clothes in front of her. "Wow. It didn't seem like all that much up until now."

"You're a lucky girl." She smiles, turning to me. "And you know something? A secret, between you and me?"

"Sure."

She leans in a little, eyes sweeping back and forth as though she's looking out for eavesdroppers before whispering, "I do a lot of these appointments. Young women come in after their man calls to confirm it's all right, and I help them pick out clothing and put it on the boyfriend's account. I have to say, you're the nicest girl I've ever worked with."

I can't help feeling a glow of pleasure. "I am?"

"Absolutely. In fact, I'd go so far as to say you're just not the type I'm used to. You're sweet and unassuming. It's nice to see a girl like you land a straight shooter like Mr. Garret. I like him and I'm glad he found such a lovely girl."

I don't have the heart to tell her I'm not his girl and that he's not entirely a straight shooter, seeing as how this is all part of a deception. Besides, it's flattering. And I need the extra confidence badly. I need to know I can convince Brock's ex that I'm the sort of girl he would have picked as his girl-friend. "Thank you," I whisper.

She moves away, all business again. "I'll have everything rung up for you. Good luck, sweetheart," she says as her assistant wheels the rack to the registers.

I feel like I should give her a tip or something, but I don't have that sort of cash on me and I suppose Brock's taking care of that, too. The sales clerks carefully package every-thing until there are six bags and three garment bags total. For one weekend? I don't even want to know what this is all coming to. More than I'd typically make in a year, maybe. It feels obscene to spend that kind of money, but it's also exhil-arating. I have to bite back a silly grin as Tom helps me load everything into the limo before whisking me off to the high-rise where Brock is waiting.

"One further thing we didn't discuss," Tom calls back as he drives.

"What's that?"

"Mr. Garret's generosity."

"You don't have to tell me about that." I laugh. My head's still spinning with the thought of all the luxurious designer clothes that are now mine. It doesn't seem real. And part of me thinks they're a waste too, because I'm never going to the kind of fancy places they would look right in. They're all way too much for a trip to the movies or the mall food court.

He's not just generous, either. He's true to his word.

Nothing Veronica chose for me is too revealing or tight. Nothing that makes me physically uncomfortable. Mentally? Ah, that's another story, but it has nothing to do with the clothing itself. It has to do with me. Even with all the work I've done on myself, all the books I've read, the seminars I've watched, the journaling, the mediation, the different tapping techniques, and every other method I've tried to get over the crap in my head from when I was a kid, my self-image is still garbage.

CHAPTER 16

Dani

"Here we are. I'll have one of the bellhops help bring the bags upstairs." Tom gets out of the car to open the door for me, then hurries inside to grab some help.

Again, I have to stop myself from telling him not to bother, that I'll manage. I need to learn how to accept help. I bet Brock's ex-girlfriend would never struggle to get all these bags upstairs by herself.

I thank the bellhop for loading everything onto a cart. Should I tip him? Jesus, pretending to be rich is a minefield. He goes inside before I can even open my purse. I exhale loudly and am about to follow him when, out of nowhere, a hand clamps around my upper arm. I barely have time to register who's manhandling me before he's in my face.

"What the fuck do you think you're doing?" he snarls.

"Luke!" And just like that my little fantasy world breaks into half. The cherry on top of my shit sundae.

His eyes are blazing with mad light.

Tom has already pulled away. Even in the middle of a crowded Manhattan sidewalk, I'm suddenly very alone. Except for my ex-boyfriend, squeezing my arm the way he used to when he was really angry for no damn reason.

"I asked you a question, Dani. What do you think you're doing? Are you living with this guy? Did you move in with him?"

"Wh—who?" I gasp, eyes wide and heart racing a mile a minute. I don't want him to hit me. Brock will not want a fiancée sporting a shiny black eye. I can't lose this job. Not for this asshole. All I have to do is keep him calm while I walk backwards. Once I'm inside the building, I don't think he would dare hit me.

"Don't ask me who. You know who. I saw you coming out of this place this morning, and I followed you to the store, then back here again. You walked out with half of Bergdorf's. What's this guy giving you?" He leans in close.

I can make out the scent of whiskey on his breath. It's just past noon, and he already smells like he's half in the bag. His dark eyes burn with rage.

I know that look. "Are you stalking me?"

He gives me a nasty smile. "No, a true stalker doesn't follow when they already know where you're going. I was waiting here for you, because I knew you would come back here. I told you before, Dani. Every breath you take, every move you make, I'll be watching you."

I freeze with shock. Is that what he's really been doing these last two months? As I stare at him in shock, he moves his face closer and tries to give me an Eskimo kiss, by rubbing his nose against mine.

"You're drunk," I say, and quickly take a step back.

He steps forward.

If I can just keep him talking and stepping forward.

"You haven't answered my question yet. Are you sleeping with him?"

"Let go of me!" I try to wrench my arm free, but it's no use. He likes feeling stronger than somebody so much smaller than him. I learned that a long time ago. But in the tussle, I manage two backward steps.

"Are you?"

"I can sleep with whoever I want, Luke. We're not together."

"We are together," he says fiercely, his hand tightening painfully on my arm. "You just wanted some breathing space, and I let you have it, but breathing space doesn't include whoring around."

This infuriates me. How many times do I have to repeat that we are freaking finished. I forget my intention to be placating. "I'm a slut, okay," I shout. "So why don't you find someone better?"

"You're not a slut," he hisses close to my face. "A slut doesn't do it for money. You're a fucking whore. You're selling yourself to him, aren't you?"

That cuts to the bone, and my face must have gone white,

because I can almost feel my blood drain away. My voice shakes. "I don't need your permission. I'll sell myself to whoever I please. Now get your stinking hands off me."

"Hey!" he shouts suddenly. Then his hand is gone from my arm as he's stumbling and trying to steady himself. A feat he only manages several feet away from me because of the strength with which Brock had shoved him.

"How dare you put your hands on her!" he roars.

In a shocked daze, I stare at Brock. The change in him is unbelievable. I'm almost terrified of him. He looks ready to kill, like an animal just looking for an excuse. He wants Luke to give him an excuse. I can just tell.

He advances on him with both hands in tight fists, tendons showing on the sides of his neck and his nostrils flaring.

"Who are you?" Luke demands.

"I'm the guy you *think* is buying her, that's who. I don't need to ask who you are. You're a filthy, small-minded little worm who doesn't understand generosity or kindness. You're less than nothing." Brock spits on the ground just by Luke's feet and sneers at him.

"And you're the asshole I'm gonna lay out flat!" Luke's swing is wide, too slow, and way too easy to block.

Brock does just that, throwing up his left arm while he takes a faster, more precise swing with his right. His fist makes contact with Luke's jaw and sends him sprawling on his back.

I can't help but let out a little scream, hands over my mouth as he hits the ground like a sack of potatoes.

Brock crouches over him, pulling him up by his jacket collar. His voice is low, menacing, but I can just make it out. "If you ever look at her again. If you ever follow her around. If you ever speak to her, call her, text her, or come within touching distance of her, I swear, I will have you killed and dumped somewhere you'll never be found. I don't think anybody would miss you." Then he casually lets go of his jacket so Luke drops with a thud.

"Did you just threaten to kill me?" Luke gasps, clutching his jaw.

"Yes." The deadly calm with which he said the word sends a shiver of fear down my spine. He really means it.

"I'll report you to the police," Luke threatens wildly.

"Do it," Brock challenges. "I don't give damn what you do, just as long as you stay away from her. Do I make myself perfectly clear?"

"Yes," Luke whispers. His eyes look like they're filling with tears as he stares up into Brock's face in shock. He's never met a man like him before. His buddies are all boys like him who never grew up, or stopped tapping kegs. Brock is a real man. Powerful in more ways than one. He might not brag about it, but he'll display it when it counts.

"Now fucking apologize to her."

Luke looks up at me. His face is full of resentment, but he obeys Brock, "I'm sorry."

I nod and rub my arm. This is all too surreal.

Brock wipes his palms on his slacks as he turns to face me. Concern replaces rage. "Are you all right?"

"Mm-hmm." I'm still too overwhelmed to speak.

"Come on. Let's go up." He wraps a protective arm around my shoulders and we walk side-by-side into the building.

I don't know what brought him outside, but I'm just so grateful he came. His arm is comforting. A reminder of how far he's willing to go to protect me. He hit Luke for me. He hurt him for hurting me. And then threatened to kill him. Nobody has ever fought my battles for me before this.

I think I'm beginning to like Brock Garret. A lot.

CHAPTER 17

Dani

Brock told me not to bother getting too dressed up for dinner. Nothing like the dress Veronica picked out for the pre-wedding dinner, but something nice. We're going to his favorite restaurant to spend a little time getting to know each other.

After that scene this afternoon, I'm not sure how to act around him.

After making sure I was okay, he suddenly took a step back from me, his body tense.

"What?" I asked him.

He shook his head and went back to work in the little study just off the living room.

Confused, I went up to my room and put my new clothes away.

A long soak in the tub, just like I'd promised myself I'd do if I ever had the chance, and a long nap made me feel like a new woman. I look at the bruise on my arm. It doesn't look good. Which reminds me that I need to do something about my hands. They look like working hands. I'll find a manicurist tomorrow.

I pick out the only woolen sheath dress from my new wardrobe. Everything we chose is better suited to Nevada weather than it is to November in New York. Low heels, thank goodness. I'm terrible in stilettos. A lot of fun I'd be in Vegas with a broken ankle. Although, I guess we could always say I did it while skiing or something equally glamorous. Do they ski in November? I have no idea.

"You're gonna be fine," I whisper to myself. Even though I still don't have anything in writing and I have no idea what I'm really getting myself into.

I sit at the mirror and start to put on my makeup. What a treat, having enough counter space for it, my curling iron and hair dryer instead of balancing it all while trying not to burn my hands off. I could get used to this sort of life. Who wouldn't?

He must have heard me coming down the stairs because he comes out of the living room and waits for me in the hallway.

The sight of him makes my heart skip a beat. He looks just as delectable as he did last night, this time wearing a black turtleneck and jacket. Black seems to be his signature color. It works well for him, setting off his eyes, which seem to glow like blue fire as he follows my progress down the stairs.

"You look…stunning." He takes a slow visual tour of my body as he speaks.

The tingle of my skin tells me I like having his eyes on me. Instead of being embarrassed, I'm pleased at his approval. He thinks I look good. "You're the one responsible for this," I remind him. "I mean, you bought it."

He shakes his head, folding his arms over his broad chest. "I'm not the one responsible. I don't believe in a Higher Power, or I didn't before I met you, but you're enough to make me second-guess my belief system."

I shake my head. "Sometimes, you're just too much."

"If only you knew."

"Whatever."

He offers his arm, and I slide mine through it before following him out the door. It feels surprisingly natural. Last night, his sense of humor shone through, but he was mainly commanding and overbearing. Tonight, he's warm and light-hearted. Maybe Luke should show up every day and stick out his chin to get popped.

The thought of him kills my smile, which Brock picks up on right away. "What's wrong? Are you thinking about him?"

I have to keep in mind how observant he is. I stare at him, amazed at how perceptive he is. "Are you psychic? We may as well get little things like this out of the way as soon as possible. It wouldn't look right for your fiancée to not know a thing like that."

"Not psychic. Just not blind."

"You looked like you enjoyed hitting him. Did you?" I ask without looking at him.

"Honestly?"

I look into his eyes. "Of course."

"Yes." His jaw tightens, as does the line of his mouth. "I enjoyed it very much. I always enjoy being able to hurt anyone who would take advantage of their power over another. He's a bully. Anyone with eyes can see it. The fact that it was you he was bullying made it even more enjoyable."

"You don't even know me."

"You're wrong about that."

I raise my eyebrows and look at him inquiringly.

Something flashes in his eyes then he says, "I might not know your favorite song, or the name of your childhood dog, or even what your favorite food is, but I know you. I knew you the moment you opened your eyes in my bed."

"Really, now? I don't know how good I feel about being so easy to read. Every woman wants to think of herself as being, I don't know, mysterious and interesting."

"I didn't say you're weren't interesting." The elevator doors open, and he throws his arm out across the doorway to keep them that way as I step out. "You're extremely interesting. You're also overworked, underpaid, ambitious, intelligent, definitely stronger than you're aware of. And you very definitely take much more shit than you deserve."

"Well," I say, my breath exhaling out in a rush. "You've

summed me up perfectly." I'm not happy about the fact that I am such an open book to him. And I don't like his smug tone.

"I forgot one or two things." The limo is waiting for us, and he waves Tom off in favor of opening the door for me.

"What's that?" I ask, waiting.

He grins. "I forgot temperamental. And gorgeous."

I roll my eyes. "Funny how that doesn't make me feel much better."

I get in the car and he closes the door behind me.

CHAPTER 18

Dani

It's a terrible habit of mine, the way I can't keep myself from checking out the prices on the menu whenever I go out to eat. It's just that I feel ridiculous ordering expensive food. A forty-dollar steak? I can buy one at the store for a quarter of the price and get three meals out of it.

Which is why the lack of prices on the menu is enough to make my skin crawl. It's just a bunch of food. No prices. I glance at Brock over the top of it. The soft overhead lights of the restaurant fall on his face making his eyebrows appear straight and black and the sweep of his eyelashes cast shadows on his cheek. His skin looks golden. I want to reach out and touch him.

"I recommend the lobster," he murmurs, before looking up and meeting my eyes.

For what seems like forever, our gazes catch and hold. The intensity of his cobalt gaze is incredible. It makes me feel exposed and vulnerable. Suddenly, there's something familiar about him. Like a dream that breaks. I blink. This is crazy. I've never met him before in my life. I don't run about in billionaire circles. I want to tear my gaze away but I can't.

Then he smiles. A lazy sexy grin and my heart starts racing. "Unless you're allergic to shellfish, of course. Are you allergic to anything, Dani?"

"Um...I can't eat strawberries," I croak. My voice sounds hoarse and thick. Why can't I breathe properly?

He nods. "I'll make a mental note of that."

I drag my gaze away and focus it on the menu. I'm actually allergic to not knowing the price of what I'm ordering. It's enough to make me break out into hives. There isn't even any chicken on the menu. It's normally a safe choice.

"What is it?" he murmurs. "You look...like you're about to self-combust."

I glance around at the tasteful décor and the low lighting, the beautiful people seated at every table. I lean forward. "Not knowing the prices of what I'm ordering is killing me."

His eyebrows rise. Then he folds his menu and hands it to me. "Here have mine. It has prices."

I take it from him and open it. My eyes almost pop out of my head. *What? A hundred and twenty dollars for a lamb burger?* I lift my gaze up to him, and he's watching me with veiled eyes. I swallow hard.

Okay, time to come clean.

"Brock, I need to tell you something. I hope it doesn't make you second-guess your decision to ask me to help you in Vegas, but I just have to honest with you."

"Okay. Spit it out."

I take a deep breath and let it out. "I don't feel like I belong here. I can't help it. I figure if we're here to get to know each other, you might as well know how insecure I am."

"That is a problem," he acknowledges with a slow nod.

"I understand if you think this was all a big mistake. I know how important it is for me to do a good job, but I'm not used to any of this and I can't help feeling like I'm out of my league."

He purses his lips, taking a deep breath.

Well, this is it. It was fun while it lasted. If I get nothing else out of the experience except the satisfaction of seeing Brock knock Luke on his butt, I'm okay with it.

Instead of breaking things off with me, however, he says, "Clearly, there a few things we need to work out between us if this has any hope of success."

"All right. I'm all ears." I place his menu off to the side and fold my hands in my lap.

One corner of his mouth quirks up in a smile. "Whatever happened to you in the past is in the past, and I would prefer you not bring it up after this. I don't mean the things we're supposed to get to know about each other, of course. If there's anything that worthless piece of shit did to you that I should be aware of before we get to Vegas, please tell me so, because I wouldn't want to cause you any undue trauma." He pauses. "Otherwise, all of that is in the past. It's no longer part of your life. Whatever your hang-ups are with regards to money, or your self-worth, put them aside and don't ever turn your attention to them again. I don't care what anybody else thinks of you. To all intents and purposes, you are the woman I have chosen to marry and if anybody makes you feel small or tries to disrespect you, they will have me to contend with."

"I wish it were that easy," I admit in a whisper.

"It is. Do you know how I know?"

I shake my head.

"Because I had to do it myself. I had a choice, early on in my life. I could either continue to be who I was, to live as I lived, to allow my family and less-than-ideal circumstances deter-mine the rest of my life. Or I could put it aside like a piece of unwanted baggage, and move on."

"Just as simple as that?"

"As simple as that. I'll let you in on a little secret." He leans in. "Nobody in this restaurant knows anything about you. They can assume, of course. You're a beautiful girl in a beautiful dress, in an exclusive restaurant with a man who's staring at you like you're the only woman in the world, because as far as I'm concerned, you are."

My heart pitter-patters. He even sounds like he means it. Why, oh why, does he have to be hung up on his stupid ex-girlfriend? Then again, I wouldn't be here if he wasn't.

"The people around you can't help but assume you're one of them. Upper-crust. High society. Big fucking deal." His smile is sexy. Dangerous. "I'll tell you something else, too."

"What?" I have to admit, he has me on the edge of my seat.

"Nobody's perfect. Everybody is neurotic in their own way. In fact, I wouldn't be surprised if these other diners whom you think *belong* in this restaurant have more insecurities than you."

"Really?"

He nods sagely. "Rich people are famously notorious for them."

"What are your insecurities, then?"

His face splits into a boyish, totally adorable grin. "Nobody's perfect but me. You didn't give me time to finish."

I can't help the loud burst of laughter that erupts from my throat. I have to cover my mouth with my hand to muffle the sound.

He laughs with me, the sound deep and infectious. "You don't need to be so serious all the time," he advises when we both stop chuckling. "I promise there's nothing on that menu I can't afford. It's not like you're wanting to burn the restaurant down, and even if you decide to do that, I could just about manage that too." He smiles at me. A wide genuine smile. "Have fun, Dani. Order something you've never tried before, and if you don't like it, you can always have something else."

I stare at him, mesmerized by the fantasy of being able to afford anything you want in life. "You're sure about this?"

"The first thing you have learn about me. I never say what I don't mean." He gestures to the menu and flashes me a roguish smile. "Go on. Live a little. Order the most expensive thing on it."

So, I do. I decide on the lobster as he suggested, and watch while he orders a bottle of wine, lapsing into French with the waiter. I can't help but thrill a little. He's so darned cultured and sophisticated. How stupid was this woman to let him slip out of her fingers? I almost can't wait to meet her.

He might have been the one to let her slip away, it occurs to me. What if he cheated on her and she left him? I watch him interacting with the waiter, occasionally glancing my way with a smile, and I decide it seems unlikely. Sure, men are men and they all have their weaknesses, but he seems like a stand-up guy. Cheating on his woman would be too tacky and ungentlemanly for him to even consider. I could be wrong, but I don't feel as though I am, and my gut is usually on point.

"What were you thinking about?" he asks, turning his attention back to me. "You smiled a little."

"One of my few happy memories as a child," I admit.

He cocks an eyebrow.

"I know you said to leave all that stuff behind, and by the way, I appreciate that very much, but I just remembered something my father told me when I was little."

His face is suddenly wary, which surprises me. "What was it?"

"That my gut would always tell me when something is right or wrong." I place a hand against my stomach. "And that I should always trust that feeling."

His gaze is steady. "What are you feeling right now?"

I check in with myself, closing my eyes for a moment. *What am I feeling?* "Good," I whisper. "I feel good." When I open my eyes again, I find him smiling in a way I haven't seen before. Ever. From anybody. Like he's looking at something he really, truly likes.

He's so handsome right now. It's enough to take my breath away. I'm liking this ex of his less and less all the time. I can't wait to get a look at her, to see what's so special that he can't move on. I wouldn't mind him moving on with me.

CHAPTER 19

Dani

The wine loosens my tongue, and by the time the food arrives, I'm babbling away like a brook. "I'm fascinated by the way the human mind works…" My voice trailing away as my eyes drink in the sight of lobster and drawn butter, asparagus with béarnaise, and potatoes au gratin. It's almost too beautiful to eat. My mouth waters, and I remember that I haven't eaten since the protein bar I scarfed down before Tom picked me up this morning. No wonder the wine and Brock's charisma seem to have gone straight to my head.

"I'm deeply interested in that myself," he agrees, as a steak is placed in front of him.

The smells from his plate are killing me. Now I wonder if I should've ordered that. Then again, he did say I could change my mind… Gosh, now I know I'm buzzed. "Oh, you are?" I pick up the knife and fork and wonder what the heck I'm supposed to do with the red crustacean in front of me.

"Don't worry," he murmurs. "I asked the waiter to have it cracked and cleaned for you. You only have to pull out the meat."

"Thank you." I take some of the claw meat and dip it delicately into the melted butter, but embarrass myself when my eyes roll back in my head. "Oh, my God."

He smiles. "It's very delicious, isn't it?" He sounds amused. Not like he's making fun of me or anything. More like he's glad to indulge a child who has been thrust into his care for a few hours.

I don't know if I like being viewed like a child, not really, but I do like being indulged. I dab at the corner of my mouth with my napkin to wipe away any butter. "They must do something very special to it. I've tasted lobster before, but this is something else,"

"Yes, you did look like you were having an orgasm over it."

"Brock!" My cheeks must be glowing as red as the poor thing's shell.

He gazes at me as he chews slowly. Even the way he chews is suggestive. "No judgment. I wish a plate of lobster could get me off that way."

I clear my throat and poke my lobster. "So what do you do?"

"What I do? I manufacture parts."

"Parts?" My nose crinkles.

"Mm-hmm."

"What kind of parts?"

"Parts for medical equipment, military equipment. Nothing very sexy."

"But I bet it's important work. You can't have medical equipment without the parts."

"True."

"But how does someone your age get to be so rich? I hope that's not a rude question, but you do seem sort of young."

He chuckles, but there's no humor there. "You're not the only one who feels that way."

I swallow the buttery asparagus in my mouth. "I didn't mean to bring up a touchy subject."

"It's all right. My grandfather owned the company, but he and my father had no relationship. I mean none whatsoever. I never even met the old man except for once when I was very young and my mother took me to see him without my father knowing. He would've had a fit if he'd found out. My grandfather was a very proud, cold man who made my mother wait outside his study while I went in and sat opposite him. I was his only grandchild. He had shrewd gray eyes and studied me closely." He frowns slightly at the memory. "I got the impression he was disappointed with what he saw, but when he died a few years ago he left me all his shares in the company, and instructions that I take his place as the CEO. If the Board didn't accept me, I had the legal right to disband the entire company as he was the majority share-holder. I was so young and the company was starting to fail, so my parents and his lawyers advised me to sell, to take the money and run. There would be enough to never have to work again."

I'm so totally enthralled with his story I stop eating, to listen.

He shrugs. "But I didn't want to do that. I suppose others in my place would have. But I wanted to make a success of things. I guess, I never forgot the disappointment in his face that one time we met. I wanted to show him…"

"That was very brave of you."

He smiles. "I don't like anybody to tell me I can't do something. It just makes me more determined than ever to do it and do it better than anybody else. I've managed to do well with the company. Taken it to new heights that no one thought it was capable of."

"I admire you," I blurt out. To the point where I haven't taken a bit of food since he started talking about how he got rich. Everything I've assumed about him seems to be adding up. He has a lot of class and a lot of character. He could've loafed around for the rest of his life, but he chose to work instead. I wish I didn't like him so darn much. Though, liking him will make it easier to pretend to be his fiancée.

"Thank you." He smiles before motioning to my plate. "Go on. Before it gets cold."

"Yes, sir," I mutter with a smirk.

"That sort of talk is unnecessary outside the bedroom."

I feel my cheeks go red again.

"Sorry. I can't help myself. You bring it out in me," he apologizes, not looking sorry at all as he cuts a piece of steak and puts it between those sinfully sexy lips.

"Yes, I'm sure you're just an innocent schoolboy, otherwise," I retort.

"As pure as the driven snow." Then he grins. "Mmm. I'm nearly as enamored with this as you are with your dinner."

"Aged beef. I've never heard of such a thing," I admit.

He points to the slab of beef with his eyebrows raised.

"All right," I say, thinking that he will cut off a piece and place it on my bread plate.

What he does is cut off a piece and brings the glistening morsel to my mouth. "You won't believe your taste buds," he murmurs, his eyes fixed on my mouth.

Is it hot in here? I have no choice but to open my mouth. The meat slides in. Somehow, the action is so sexual and full of lust, I have to close to my eyes to block out the sight of his blue, blue eyes and the strange expression in them so that I can concentrate on tasting the meat.

It's like butter, practically melting on my tongue. It has a flavor I didn't know existed in anything, especially not steak. After I get control of myself, yes, I managed not to groan like I did over the lobster, I open my eyes and shake my head. "Until a few years ago, I was convinced that I hated steak."

"Why is that?" he asks, a half-smile on his face.

"Because my foster mother's idea of cooking steak was slapping it down on the pan and going into the other room to check the weather forecast. She didn't pay any attention to it. It wasn't ready to eat until you could bounce it off the floor." Even now the memory of meat burning makes me shudder. "I can still remember sitting there, chewing and chewing and trying to get it down my throat because of the *finish every-thing on your plate* rule we had in the house. Ugh, it was nasty. Like eating leather. Needless to say, I couldn't understand why anyone would ever order beef at a restaurant."

"Reminds me of my mother's cooking." He chuckles. "She tried. She really did, but instead of making something simple, like spaghetti and meatballs, which, incidentally, is my favorite meal, she was always trying to make these extravagant dishes that would fail magnificently. But of course, we all had sit at the table and pretend it was good."

I smile at the thought of him as a small boy. "You can afford to eat like this, but your favorite dish is spaghetti and meatballs?"

"Oh, hell, yeah. And a good peanut butter and jelly sandwich is my weakness." He winks. "Another something you should know."

Those days when we had peanut butter and jelly sandwiches for dinner every damn day flash into my head, but I smile pleasantly. "You're a man of mystery, Brock."

"You have no idea." His eyes are inscrutable over the rim of his wine glass.

It's the nicest dinner I've ever had in my entire life, but the funny thing is, it would've been even if we'd eaten drive-thru burgers. It was special because of him.

CHAPTER 20

Dani

I slip into my nightgown. Pale pink satin. It supposed to be for Vegas, but I couldn't resist the lure of it. I look at myself in the mirror. It's perfect with my chocolate hair. I feel downright dangerous in it.

It must be the wine, still making my blood pump hotter and faster than usual.

What is it about him, about this penthouse, about this night that makes me feel so sexy? I might as well be a different person. Sure, Luke and I slept together. Not a lot thought. He was pretty much always in the mood, but between work and school I was always tired.

Never once have I ever felt like this.

Sensuous, alive and intensely aware of my body in ways I've

never been before. Even the way I move is different. I notice it when I walk past the full-length mirror. Who is this woman? She's so confident. So sure of herself. She even sways her hips as she walks. I move closer, examining the way the satin skims my curves like water flowing over me. I can't stop touching it, it's so soft and silky.

My cheeks are still flushed from the wine. I need some water if I'm going to get away without feeling like hell tomorrow. There's a matching robe on the foot of the bed, which I belt firmly before going towards the stairs.

Brock's bedroom door is closed. I imagine him in bed and wonder what he's wearing. Does he own pajamas, or does he sleep in his boxers? Or does he go to bed naked? My nipples harden before I can keep the thoughts at bay.

I can only blame this on the wine for so long.

It's better for me to hurry downstairs, get my water and get to bed. The worst thing I can do right now is think about him that way, even if it will help my performance over the weekend. It will only hurt to give him up when it's all over if I start developing feelings for him.

Downstairs, it's silent and still. With the almost all of the lights off, except a few wall sconces. I walk through the dim spaces and go to the kitchen. It is like a sanctuary, lit only by the light over the stove. I wonder if this room ever even gets used. Brock doesn't seem like the type to cook for himself. Who would in his position? I haven't seen any staff around the place, though I suppose there could be when he's hosting a dinner party or something.

I walk quickly across the cold marble floor, my feet hardly making any sound, and open the fridge. To my surprise, it is stuffed full with all kinds of food. When I was cleaning it yesterday, there was nothing in it except some lemons, bottles of champagne, water, and tonic. I wonder if it's for my benefit. Surely not.

It's probably a good idea to take two bottles, so I do before heading back to the stairs. A gust of air blows my robes against my legs, and I shiver. Is this apartment really that drafty? I look around for the source of the air and, gasp when I find it.

There he is, standing on the balcony with his back to me, looking out over the city. My heart starts thudding against my ribcage. He looks so unapproachable, so insular. What must it be like to be as powerful as he is? He probably feels like a king, standing there looking down over his kingdom. I try to imagine what must be running through his head.

Maybe he's thinking about her.

About watching her get married this weekend. Something twinges in my chest. Jealousy. I wish I was her. What it must be like to have a man like him pining for me? He's been good to me. I can't help but warm to him. Actually, it's more than that, but I don't think too much about exactly how I feel about him. So I'll just call it gratitude. I'm grateful to him. He's been kind and supportive and generous, heaven knows. He doesn't have to do half of what he's done for me so far. The clothes, maybe even the food in the fridge. The over the top payment and I don't even want to know what he spent on tonight's dinner.

I know I should leave him there.

I should go upstairs and forget I ever saw him standing there with the city lights illuminating his body. There's tension in his shoulders and back like he's thinking about something that doesn't make him very happy. I have to go out there and at least try to make him feel better. I owe him that much, at least.

He turns his head when I say, "Hey."

CHAPTER 21

Dani

"Can't sleep?" His voice is neutral, and his face in the shadows, so I can't make out his expression.

"I came down for something to drink and wondered if you were all right, standing out here like this." Dang, it's chilly. Downright cold. My nipples are like rocks when I reach him and I'm suddenly very aware of the thin satin between my skin and the night air. And him. Crossing my arms over my chest helps.

"You'll catch cold out here," he warns softly.

"So will you."

"I'm not half-naked."

"Neither am I, the last time I checked. I'm fully covered. And thank you, by the way."

"For?"

"For this, for everything. I didn't need nightgowns, you know. I brought my own. And no one is going to see them."

"It'll be better for you to live in the role."

"Rich girls dress like this for bed?"

"Some do." He turns to me, leaning against the railing.

"Am I doing all right as your fiancée so far?"

He nods slowly. "If you carry on doing this good, you'll end up convincing me that you are my fiancée."

"Ha, ha," I say, but my heart skips a beat.

"Is being my fiancée what you thought it would be?"

"I've never been engaged, so I don't have anybody to compare you to..." I grin. "But you're doing fine. Better than I could've expected."

"Really? Even though I've never given you an engagement ring?"

"Oh, my gosh!" I gasp, forgetting about covering my chest as my hands fly to my mouth. "I forgot."

"I guessed you had." He chuckles. "But I didn't. My fiancée deserves an audaciously, insanely expensive ring."

"But I would never—"

"...Feel comfortable wearing something like that," he finishes. "Yes, I know. But this coming weekend isn't about you, is it? And it isn't about your comfort."

"I thought you said you'd never make me wear something that would make me feel uncomfortable?" I tease.

His eyes twinkle. "I think we agreed to no porn star fetish clothes. But I don't remember any discussions about impressive rings."

I shrug. "Okay. Why not? It's all pretend, anyway. I don't know what I'm thinking. You're being so generous. Thank you."

He slides a hand into the back pocket of his pants.

I gape at him. "Wait. Now? I didn't think you were going to give it to me now!"

"Give it to you?" He arches an eyebrow. "I love it when you talk dirty."

"Or maybe I'm not talking dirty, you just have a nasty mind." *Whoa. Did I just say that?*

I guess I did, since his smile widens, and grows more wicked. "It's all your fault. I feel downright filthy whenever you're around."

"Down, boy." I giggle, flushing all over.

"You're right, of course. This is a very serious event." He clears his throat, wiping all traces of a smile off his face. "I'm asking my fake fiancée to marry me, after all."

"This is the most romantic situation of my entire life," I deadpan.

He bursts out laughing. "You're ruining the moment I've been carefully practicing for a lifetime."

I mime zipping my lips shut and throwing the key over the balcony.

"Dani Saber will you be my fake fiancée this weekend?"

"Yes. A million times, yes." I clutch my hands together like a princess in a Disney movie, and flutter my eyelashes as if I'm about to swoon.

A wry smile lifts one corner of his mouth. "All right, smart ass. Here you are." He pulls out the small, velvet box and flips it open to reveal a ring which makes my jaw drop.

It sparkles like a star from a dark surface. My heart stops for a second. I reach for it, then I pull my hand back.

"Why did you do that?" he asks, taking the ring from the box.

"Do what?"

"You pulled back at the last moment."

"I—I, nothing."

"You wanted it didn't you?"

I cross my arms and shrug. "It's a very beautiful ring. That would have been a normal reaction for any woman."

He stares at me. "No it was more than that. It stirred something in you, didn't it? You denied yourself what you want in the depths of your heart." He smiles gently. "Rightly so, seeing as how it was one of the rings I liked best when I went to Tiffany's today."

"You said you had to work."

"Buying a ring is work for me," he says dryly. He takes my hand and holds it up, positioning the ring at my fingertip. "I must warn you; this ring isn't one of the things you can keep. It's on loan."

"I understand." I wouldn't even know what to do with it once I got home, anyway. What would I do with a zillion carat emerald-cut diamond? The insurance alone would bankrupt me.

He pushes the band along my finger. Once the cool platinum band is in place, he pats the back of my hand, in an almost fatherly gesture.

I look up at him and our eyes lock as all of a sudden—the mood changes. How freaking bizarre, but this doesn't feel fake. I must be going mad. The wine. Of course, the wine. Obviously, this isn't real. He clearly said, the ring has to go back.

He raises my hand to his lips. "You deserve a ring like this," he whispers, his breath warm against my skin. "And you deserve to know what it feels like to not hold yourself back from what you want deep in your heart."

I can't breathe. I'll never breathe again. *God, why can't this be real? Why can't I really have something like this? Someone like him?*

He lowers my hand and looks deep into my eyes, moving closer until the warmth of his body and the scent of his skin are the only things in the world. Not even the massive engagement ring matters right now. Nothing does except Brock and the web of breathless desire he's weaving around me.

When he catches my lower lip between his own, I lean into the kiss and let him wash over me. I can't believe this. It's not just a kiss—oh, no. That would be like comparing the piece of meat he gave me at dinner to the steak I grew up eating. It's on an entirely different level. An entirely different plane of existence. His mouth on mine, moving slowly. Drawing it out. Making me groan from a place deep down in my center, a place only he's ever been able to touch. All through one simple, firm but gentle kiss.

It stays gentle for only so long.

When he knows how darn affected I am, his hands slide around my waist until they're pressing into my back and pulling my body closer to his. I feel him so acutely through the satin, and he can feel me. My skin warms at his touch and I wind my arms around his neck to hold on as he slowly drives me crazy and my knees go too weak to keep me standing. His tongue slides along the opening of my mouth before probing inside, exploring me as fireworks go off in my head. He groans, his hands pressing harder, the need between us growing like a fire which threatens to consume us both.

I want it to.

Yes, I want it with every fiber of my being. I want his hands on me and his lips, oh, his lips, his tongue and all of it. All of him. All night long and into the morning, again and again. I want to touch him everywhere and taste his skin and listen as he whispers my name in the darkness. My entire body seems to sizzle, and my nerve endings feel like they dancing and singing. Every cell in my body is desperate for satisfaction. But no. There will be none tonight.

I can't.

We can't.

My eyes fly open.

It takes every ounce of strength in my body and soul to pull away. It has to be done. We can't take this any further, because he loves somebody else. He still loves her. Whoever she is. And I won't be the woman who gets used and hurt. Not like this. Not when I know his heart is pining for another woman and I'm just a body in the dark.

He's breathing heavily, nearly panting, and his erection is so strong I fear it will break the zipper of his slacks. I'm already wet, was from the moment our lips met, but the sight of his hard on makes me crave him inside me.

"We can't do this." I gasp, shaking my head, stepping away, hoping the cool night air will take away some of the burning in my cheeks. Maybe it will cool me off, too.

"Dani, wait a second."

"No. Please don't. You're in love with another woman. We have an arrangement and it doesn't include sex. I'm sorry if I gave you the impression I was available. I don't drink much and all that wine went straight to my head." I manage a wobbly smile. "I did really have a good time tonight though. Thank you for that."

"You're welcome, but—"

"I should go back inside now. To sleep." I can't look at him anymore. If I do, he'll pull me under again and I might not be able to make my way up to the surface this time. I want him too badly.

He doesn't try to stop me. He's forceful, but he knows how to take no for an answer.

125

"One more thing." I stop, turning my head to the side. "I would like for our agreement to be put in writing and signed by the two of us before we leave on Friday morning. I want to be sure the terms are set in stone before we go."

"Of course." He's all business now. There's none of that breathless lust in his voice anymore.

Good thing. Neither of us needs it.

CHAPTER 22

DANI

"Everything in order?" He nearly vibrates with impatience as he waits for me to go through the contract he's drawn up. It is a simple agreement. No lawyer jargon and no room for misunderstanding. Basically, I agree to do my best to convince everybody of the charade that we are engaged and in return, I get the money. There's also a bunch of information about how the money will be transferred to me, and that all seems to line up.

"Yes, this seems to cover everything," I say softly.

I sign beneath his signature on both copies while his bespectacled lawyer, who had stood next to him with a poker face, witnesses the signing.

I put the pen down and look up.

There is a satisfied smile on Brock's face.

He presses a button in the panel beside his seat. "Let's get rolling."

The pilot confirms his order and within moments, the jet starts moving.

I run my hands, my nails all glossy with overlays over the soft seats and admire the luxury surrounding me. I didn't know a jet could be like this. It's more like a hotel than anything else. Aside from the seats, which are of course necessary, there are two bedrooms and a conference room.

He showed me around before we took our seats and reviewed the contract. He was very businesslike about it.

I suspect it has to do with the way I refused him on Tuesday night, but I couldn't help it. I still think it was the best decision for both of us. We would've only complicated things if we'd taken things any further. Sure, it sucked. Hard. And it still sucks while I can't stop wondering what would've happened if I hadn't stopped it. How incredible it would've been...

But no.

This is a business arrangement, plain and simple. No point breaking my heart over something I plainly can never have. I made the right choice. If his ego is a little hurt, there's nothing I can do about that, but settle in and get ready for the weekend. It's a good thing I don't naturally get airsick, because my stomach is already twisted in knots at the thought of what I'll face when we arrive.

I don't have to wait long before finding out exactly what I'm up against.

The hotel is dazzling, and I slide my sunglasses up until they rest on top of my head, so I can get a good look around. In the interest of research and not looking like a fish out of water, I've already read everything I could about the Mandarin Oriental.

It is certainly as amazing as the articles and reviews I read. The soaring ceilings of the lobby, the gold and deep red accents, the shining black marble. It's exquisite. I feel like a princess as Brock and I walk in, arm-in-arm.

"It's showtime, baby," he murmurs.

"What if I do something wrong?"

"Then I'll have to punish you."

"I'll tell you right now: my safe word is *get off*!"

He smiles slowly and wickedly.

I wish he'd take off his glasses so I can see what he's really thinking. I hope he doesn't plan on freezing me out all weekend when we're alone, the way he's done these last few days, except for the times when we were brushing up on our knowledge of each other and our made-up relationship.

I make a point of leaning against him a little and making sure my ring faces straight ahead.

"Ah, yes. Mr. Garret." The concierge nearly falls over himself when he realizes who he's speaking to. "And this must be your lovely fiancée."

"Yes, this is Miss Saber."

Out of sheer habit, I hold out a hand to greet him. Karl, according to his name badge. Then I withdraw it quickly when I see the surprise on his face. Shit. I glance up quickly at Brock to see if he noticed my faux pas, but he only smiles down indulgently at me.

"I hope you enjoy your visit, Miss Saber. The Mandarin Suite is all ready for you both. If you need anything, please don't hesitate to ask. There is no need to register at the reception."

Well, well, how the rich live.

He nods to one of the bellhops who immediately loads up our bags, and we follow behind the cart to the bank of elevators just beyond the desk.

"Brock?"

I feel him freeze at the sound of a high-pitched, almost squealing female voice. I freeze too, but immediately fall into fiancée mode. I have a job to do. I turn my head slightly. The tall, leggy blonde rushing across the lobby with her arms extended has to be the woman I've been brought here to make jealous.

She's gorgeous, like something off a runway. She might as well be walking down one as she struts around in a designer sundress with—surprise, surprise—the sky-high heels Brock said I didn't need to wear if I didn't want to. Her hair sparkles like gold as she tosses it over one tanned shoulder. Her green eyes glow with happiness. At least, she wants us to think it's happiness, but there is something false about her.

"I didn't think you would come. I really didn't." She flashes him a brilliant smile as her hands land on his shoulders, in spite of the fact that I'm still holding onto his arm and his hand is in mine. She has perfectly balanced, delicate features with full, glossy lips which she puckers as though she's waiting for a kiss that never comes.

Oh, I hate her.

"Dani, this is Charlotte." Brock looks down at me with a smile. He doesn't even stop looking at me for the rest of the introduction. "Charlotte, this is Dani."

I squeeze his arm and drop a quick wink. We've got this, I want to tell him. I hope he knows. This woman is clearly a nightmare, I can tell just by looking at her. She's high-maintenance, shrill, and doesn't care that he's clearly with another woman. Although she left him, she'll touch him when she wants to and act as if she is still the only woman in the world that's important to him. And that's just to spite me.

I can just imagine what a debacle this wedding is going to be.

Even so, she's beautiful and classy in her way, and much more sophisticated than I am. She wears her designer outfit like it's a second skin, while I feel like an imposter. I almost feel sorry for Brock, having to pretend he's not still in love with her. Having to pretend he's in love with me.

"Dani. What a...charming name? I wasn't aware Brock was bringing anyone along with him, but this is very sweet." She smiles brilliantly at me, and it truly feels as though the sun just broke through the clouds to shower me with light. She's enchanting.

Maybe I'm the one who is being jealous and catty and she's a genuinely nice person who is also flawlessly beautiful. That would explain why Brock is still so in love with her. My smile mirrors hers. I hope. "I thought I might have to work this weekend, but managed to reschedule my appointments at the last minute. I hope I'm not inconveniencing you in any way?"

"Not at all. It's a pleasure to have you here," she says graciously.

"I couldn't be here without my fiancée," Brock murmurs, kissing my earlobe.

I giggle before turning his way, and standing on tiptoe to kiss him for real. I don't expect it to be anything more than a basic kiss, just for show. I'm wrong. God, how wrong.

He takes the side of my face in his hand and plunges his tongue into my mouth, swirling it around until my head is whirling and my toes are nearly curling. By the time he pulls away, my heart is beating a mile a minute, and I feel more than a little giddy.

What was that all about? I thought he wasn't a fan of public displays of affection. He must really want to show her.

I turn to Charlotte with the intention of apologizing for the sudden show and see something that takes my breath away... all over again.

She looks furious. Beyond furious. She's trying to hide it, trying to smile like she did before, but she fails miserably. Her face looks brittle, like it might crack into a million pieces. Her eyes are cold and hard.

Oh, my Lord!

I don't know if Brock sees it, but I do. She still desperately wants Brock and hates me for being with him. What the heck does she care? She's getting married this weekend! There goes any hope of her being a gracious loser and remembering that this is her weekend and we're all here for her.

"We should get up to the suite," Brock announces, sliding an arm around my waist and steering me toward the elevators.

I sense the urgency in him. He wants to get away from her. I don't blame him, I want the same thing, but for different reasons. He's afraid she'll know he's still in love with her. I think she's a nightmare. I was willing to give her a break until I saw that look on her face.

"Come to lunch with us!" she calls out.

We stop and look at each other. I still can't see his eyes, so I can't tell what he thinks about this. But his arm tightens.

"I don't know. We just landed and I know I'd like Dani to relax a little," he says, looking at Charlotte over the top of my head.

Her next question is directed at me, "You're not tired, are you, Dani?"

"Um…"

"See? She's not. Oh, come on, don't be such a spoilsport. I would love for you to meet Trent."

Trent? Yeah, that sounds like the perfect name for the sort of guy who would marry her.

"Please? We're having lunch here at the restaurant, in an hour. You can't deny the bride, the day before her wedding." She tilts her head to the side and pouts.

Ugh. She's insufferable.

"Sure," Brock capitulates with a shrug. "Sure, we'd love to."

He really has it bad for her if he can't see what a manipulative little bitch she is.

I wish I could get away with slugging him.

CHAPTER 23

DANI

B rock hands the patient bellhop some folded-up cash
and waits until the door is closed behind us before
speaking, "Clearly, there was nothing I could do about that."

"Clearly. But what about sticking your tongue down my
throat?" I ask, hands on my hips. "What was that all about?"

"I might have gotten a little caught up in the moment." He
avoids looking at me, choosing instead to explore the suite.
"She needs to know who you are to me."

"Who I'm *supposed* to be, you mean."

"Of course," he says smoothly.

I sit on the edge of the bed and look around the suite. It's
simply stunning. There are two bedrooms, both with king-
sized beds, a living and dining room. I can see into the bathroom from where I'm sitting and the sunken tub looks out
over the strip through the windows that surround it. "This is
gorgeous," I say, running my hands over the ultra-soft
bedspread. It reminds me of falling asleep on Brock's bed

and everything that led to this moment. Has it really only been four days? Not even.

"It's the best suite with two bedrooms in this place," he informs me. Leaning against the open door, he takes off his cufflinks and rolls up his sleeves.

How the heck does he make a button-down and khaki slacks look so darn sexy?

"I hope you'll be comfortable here."

I chuckle. "There would have to be something seriously wrong with me if I couldn't find comfort here."

"That's why I know you're perfect for this," he murmurs. His glasses are off and I can see honesty in his eyes. "Thank you again, by the way."

"Thank you. I could never have a weekend like this on my wages. I know you said to leave that stuff behind, but it's the truth. This?" I wave my arms around, then motion toward my clothes and sandals. "I could never make this happen on my own."

"By the time this weekend is over, you might not be thanking me. So I'll accept any thanks while you're willing to offer it."

"That sounds pretty ominous. Are you trying to scare me?"

"You saw what she's like. Impossible to deny, someone who always gets her way through sheer force of will. And now, we have to sit at lunch with her and her fiancé."

There's so much darkness in his voice, so much emotion, my heart goes out to him. I wish he would get over her. My stomach fills with resentment. She's not that spectacular, for God's sake.

But I guess, so much more spectacular than I could ever hope to be. And she has one more advantage over me—she has his heart.

The restaurant is just as beautiful as the rest of the hotel and very fancy. Not to mention filled with gorgeous people. It's definitely not the sort of place I've heard about, the cheap buffets and windowless rooms where gamblers can't tell if it's day or night.

This is a totally different world. The midnight-blue ceiling is two-stories high while lit glass orbs hang suspended from thin cords throughout the room, giving the impression of luminous moons in the night sky. I can just imagine how much more lovely it would be at night, with the view of the Las Vegas strip outside the windows. It will be like dining in the sky.

Charlotte waves at us from her table.

My eyes immediately shift to the man sitting with her. He looks every inch like the kind of man I imagined she'd marry. He even pops the collar on his polo shirt and wears his sunglasses on the back of his head when he's not using them. Holy jeez. She went from Brock to this guy? What's her problem? Is she that desperate? No, she can't be. Women like her don't get desperate.

I squeeze Brock's hand to let him know I'm with him in this, and he squeezes back. I wonder what he must be feeling right now. Insulted, if he's got even a grain of sense. I know I would be. We're both all smiles, though, when we reach the table.

"This is Trent," Charlotte beams, introducing us both in turn. Brock extends his hand in greeting, which Trent shakes seemingly as an afterthought while checking something on the phone in his other hand. He doesn't greet me. He doesn't even look at me.

"So, you two." Charlotte rests her elbows on the table, her chin nestled in her hands. "Tell me the story! How long have you been together?" She flashes a fake smile. "I didn't even know Brock had a new girlfriend!"

"How would you know?" Brock points out. We're sitting at a square table, one of us on either side, with Brock to my left. He makes a point of linking his fingers with mine on top of the table...in plain view.

She pouts sensuously at him.

Oh, how I want to slap her.

"Mark, of course. I expect Mark to tell me when something this important happens."

Okay, I have to jump in here. "You know Brock and Mark. They'll talk about business until the cows come home before switching it over to how Mark's fantasy football team is doing. God forbid, they talk about anything important." I give his arm a playful smack.

At this, his eyebrows fly upwards. "Besides," he adds, "I was trying to be a gentleman. I asked him not to mention anything about us to you. It's in poor taste to rub a relationship in an ex's face. Don't you think?"

She purses her lips and looks away, to where Trent is still on his phone. She very deliberately pulls his hand away from it and holds it in her own.

The romance is just flowing between these two. If they're in love, I'm a unicorn.

The waiter comes and she looks up at him, the simpering expression dying from her face. "Plain salad with grilled chicken. A lemon wedge instead of dressing. Make a note to the chef to cut out all the fat from the chicken before grilling."

I order a salad too, but a normal one with chicken, berries, and glazed nuts.

"Make sure there are no strawberries, though," Brock tells the waiter.

I turn to stare at him, amazed that he remembered.

He looks into my eyes and touches my nose gently. "I wouldn't want you coming out in hives," he murmurs.

"Thank you," I whisper, before dragging my eyes away from his and turning to face Charlotte. I feel almost hypnotized by him.

She is watching us avidly. She smiles tightly. "I wish I could eat whatever I wanted right now, the way you can, but fitting into that dress tomorrow…well you'll know all about it soon enough."

I glance at Brock. "I'm sure I will."

"How did you two love birds meet?" she asks eagerly.

I smile. "Well, I own several house cleaning businesses in Manhattan, and Brock reached out to us. I like to meet our high-profile clients in person, you know, get to know them a little better before being certain that our services are right for them."

"And it was love at first sight," Brock adds.

The tenderness in his voice makes my head whirl around in surprise, searching his face. If I didn't know any better, I'd swear he meant it. He winks at me and I realize he's just acting. He must really want to put the screws to Charlotte.

Charlotte tilts her head to the side, frowning. If her forehead wasn't so Botoxed, she'd be able to create some lines, but no such luck. "So you're a housekeeper?" she asks, deliberately misunderstanding.

I make my voice saccharine sweet. "No, dear. I own the business." She'd better not try to Google my name, or I'm screwed. I hadn't thought about her challenging me like this.

Brock clearly didn't consider it, either. "What about you?" he asks, breaking in, looking from Charlotte to Trent.

"Huh?" It's literally the first sound the man has made outside of ordering a burger and fries. And another whiskey.

"You're the real love birds here." I grin. "The big day is tomorrow, there's a huge party in your honor tonight. We want to hear more about you two. How did you meet? How did Trent propose?"

"Oh, it's the sweetest story ever. Can I tell it, honey?" Charlotte coos.

"What? Yeah. Sure." He barely glances up at her.

Brock coughs to cover up a laugh, but it's a pretty poor attempt. I can see right through him, and so can Charlotte.

She decides to kick things up a notch, running her fingers through Trent's hair like she's grooming him. There is no tenderness or affection between them.

Well, this is how she wants to play it? Okay. I lean against Brock a little too. It's a much more natural gesture than anything the two of them have exchanged so far. I actually feel comfortable being this close to him.

"We were in Paris…" She sighs, closing her eyes for a moment. "At the top of the Eiffel Tower, it was so romantic."

"Paris? It sounds very romantic," I mumble.

Brock gives me a gentle kick under the table.

I kick him back. It's either that or burst out laughing at how ridiculous this is.

She fixes me with a shrewd glare. "Oh? You've never been to Paris, have you?"

Shit. She's smarter than I gave her credit for. "No," I admit. "Which is why it seems so romantic to me. It probably isn't as romantic in real life as I have it built up in my head."

Another fake cough from Brock.

Her eyes narrow as she looks from my innocent face to Brocks' politely blank expression. "Anyway," she continues with a shake of her golden tresses. "There we were. At the top of the tower. And he got down on one knee and proposed and there was champagne and flowers and everybody around us clapped. It was one of those perfect moments."

"Aww…that so sweet," I say, and give myself an A+ for sounding so genuine.

"What about you two?" she asks, arching an eyebrow. Her eyes are sharp and watchful.

Brock clears his throat. "Ah, we were out on the balcony at my place. So, not as grand a gesture as Trent's. To be honest, I had a different plan, but I couldn't help myself." He turns to gaze at me with sheep's eyes. "There she was standing in her nightgown, shivering, and I couldn't wait one second longer…"

Oh, my God, he is a far, far better actor that I gave him credit for. I was there, so I know that's not how it went down, but hell, his version is so much better.

He nods at me.

Now, I know that it's my turn to carry the torch. "Yeah, you warmed me up," I say in an awed voice.

Something flashes behind his eyes. Then a slight smile touches his mouth and suddenly, I remember that mouth and what it did to me, what I wanted it to do.

"And you said it was the most romantic moment of your life." He grins.

I burst out laughing because yes, I did say that.

We laugh together. For that moment, we're not actors—we are actually joined by a secret memory.

Charlotte clears her throat.

I tear my gaze away from his sparking blue eyes and face her. "Oh, it might not have been Paris, but it was very memorable." I admire my ring. "A girl doesn't forget a night like that."

Charlotte chuckles. "Remember when we went to Paris, Brock?" Her voice is deep with meaning.

I want to stab her with my fork. She'll make a beautiful bride with one of her eyes gouged out. Maybe she can find a diamond-encrusted eye patch.

"Did we go to Paris? I can't remember," Brock replies.

Our food arrives then, and Charlotte uses it as an excuse to change the subject back to herself. She has plenty of bragging to do about her silly wedding plans if she's going to make up for the burn Brock just delivered.

I'm proud of him. He's handling this so well. It even seems like he's having fun. As much fun as a person can have while getting their teeth pulled out, that is. This entire lunch feels like a trip to the dentist's office.

It's only when we're alone in the elevator that either of us breathes a little easier. "You did brilliantly well," he declares.

"Thank you. For the record, so did you."

He runs a hand through his hair and I see the man behind the façade. Oh, sure, he's handsome, cultured, sophisticated, wealthy and powerful, but he's also a real person with real feelings. And seeing her with her new man—no matter how little he seems to care that they're getting married tomorrow night—must have him a little shaken up.

"Who orders their burger well done?" I muse, leaning against the wall as we zip up to our room.

He laughs. "Yes, he's something else. I wonder where they actually met and what he does with himself all day. I noticed, she wouldn't let us ask."

"Yeah, I noticed that too." I smirk. "But nevermind, I now

know about every single hoop she had to jump through to get just the right number of white lilies for the ceremony."

"And not just white, but the correct shade of white," he adds with a chuckle.

"I didn't even know there was such a thing. I thought all lilies were white?"

"So did I," he agrees.

We step off the elevator, me first as always.

Before parting ways inside the suite, I place a hand on his arm.

He turns to me with an enquiring expression on his handsome face.

"I just want to say something, and I really need for you to not take it the wrong way."

"An interesting start," he observes.

"Please. Listen to me." It sounds stupid in my head, but I have to get it out. "I think you're a genuinely nice guy. A little rough on the outside, maybe a little difficult to get to know. But decent...and honest...and very generous. And kind too. I really think it's a real shame that Charlotte couldn't see that for herself. She made a big mistake. Trent isn't half the man you are."

He gets that look on his face again, like he had at the restaurant. A sort of...I don't know...amazement? He didn't expect me to be so serious. "Thank you for saying that. I'm deeply touched."

I nod. "It's just that I didn't want to overstep my boundaries."

"Dani, I found you sleeping in my bed. There are only a few boundaries left between us. This isn't one of them." He reaches for me, sweeping the back of his hand over my cheek and making the hair on the back of my neck stand up. "But thank you for being one of the only real, genuine women I've ever had the pleasure to know. Truly."

"You're welcome."

He smiles before taking a step back, and turning in the direction of his room. The heels of his shoes tap on the polished floor. "The rehearsal dinner starts at six. We've been invited. The party's after that."

Oh. Goody. Because having lunch with them wasn't enough. His door closes with a soft click, and I look out over the strip, as I go over the little moments since we got here. The looks she gave the two of us, especially after that kiss in the lobby. The digs during lunch. The way she kept bringing up my healthy appetite, now that I think about it—five times in total. Like I'm a pig for eating a salad with dressing on it. Her insinuation that I'm a cleaning woman, which I am, of course, but she's not supposed to know that. So how dare she just assume. Stuck up, bitch!

Oh, it makes my blood boil.

She's going to see what I'm capable of when I put my mind to it. She's not the only one who can play mind games.

"Brock?" I go over to his closed door, and rap on it smartly with my knuckles.

"Yes?"

"Do you mind if I get my hair done for tonight? There's a salon downstairs."

He opens the door, and my eyes widen. His shirt is pulled out of his pants and unbuttoned all the way to his waist. And wow! Did someone say washboard abs! Reluctantly, I pull my eyes up to his face. He is holding his phone so I guess I must have interrupted a phone call.

"Of course not," he says. "Shoot the works, whatever you want. Charge it to the room."

"*Thanks,*" I mouth silently, because quite honestly, I feel robbed of sound.

He nods and closes the door again.

I exhale slowly. Oh, my God, the man is a Greek god. Taking a deep breath, I grin to myself. He said yes. Just you wait Charlotte. By the time this night is finished, you'll see how stupid you were to let him go, and you'll also know I'm no one to be played with either.

Brock deserves to have someone fighting in his corner.

And that someone is me.

CHAPTER 24

Brock

"Sorry. Just Dani," I say into the phone as I slide out of my shirt, and toss it onto the bed.

"When do I get to meet this goddess then?" Mark asks.

"You'll see her tonight, at dinner."

"You're coming to that?"

"Charlotte demanded it," I say dryly.

"Oh, yeah, right. Since when have you done what Charlotte wanted?"

"Since it suits my interests."

"Hmmm…that reminds me. Charlotte's really swinging for the fences, isn't she?"

I laugh when I remember the way she pawed at her so-called

fiancé, trying everything but a lap dance to get his attention. "I don't think I've ever seen a guy less interested in getting married. He seemed uninterested in anything but his phone...and the popped collar of his shirt."

"Tool?"

"Definitely."

"How's your girl doing?"

"Honestly, much better than I imagined. I thought she might be a little stiff at first, but she loosened up right away. I think she has a hidden competitive streak, and Charlotte set her off at the get go."

"How could she not? She's the Queen of Competitiveness," he snorts. "She brings it out in everybody."

"Not me. Maybe because she wasn't worth competing over."

"I take it you think Dani is, though."

"I wouldn't say that." I keep my voice mild. If Mark knew how far I would go for Dani...

"No? So you gave her asshole ex that little love tap, because you wanted to practice your right hook?"

"I knocked him on his ass because he deserved it. Any man who handles a woman that way deserves what he gets."

"Fair enough." He pauses. "Would you have done it for Charlotte?"

"Yes, if anybody had touched Charlotte like that when we were together, I would've knocked him out too."

"Also fair. But that's my point. You just compared the two of them like they're on equal footing. They're not. Unless I had too much too drink that night we met at the bar and misunderstood the situation, Dani's *not* your actual girlfriend."

I stand at the window and look down at the strip. "I know that."

"You're sure about that?"

I turn away from the window. I need to end this call. "Is this one of your pathetic attempts at busting my balls? You're not good at it."

"If I wasn't good at it, you wouldn't hate it." He laughs. "Are you ever gonna tell her?"

I feel my body still. "Tell her what?"

"You know what. What this is really all about. How you don't care about Charlotte and only brought her with you under false pretenses. Or were you planning on leading her on indefinitely?"

"I wouldn't say I'm leading her on."

"Oh, no?"

"No. She's getting the money. She's getting the weekend. I'm not lying to her about that."

"No. Not about that."

"Look, I don't have time for this. Why don't you focus on your duties as best man, instead of giving me shit?"

"All right, all right. I'll back off. I can tell when I've hit a nerve. I'll see you tonight."

Damn him. One of the drawbacks to having a lifelong friend

is the way they can see right through you. He knows me too well to let me get away with bullshit. No, I don't know exactly how this is all going to end with her, or what she's going to do when she finds out this was all under false pretenses. I only know that she has to be mine. I've known it since I saw her in my bed.

No. That's not true. Even before then.

In the schoolyard. I was a kid, and I didn't have a clue about the way of the world, but I knew I wanted her even then. I don't know where the certainty came from, either. But it was there. Always. The certainty that she was it for me. Now that I've found her again, and I know what she's grown into, I'm never letting her go.

"Come on. We're going to be late," I remind her from my spot by the front door for perhaps the third time. My blood pressure is on the rise.

"I'm sure they won't mind even if we're a few minutes behind," she calls out from her bedroom. "Besides, it's not like we have far to go. It's right downstairs. Unless there's an elevator traffic jam..."

"All right, all right, smartass. But if we're going to do this together, one thing you need to know: I detest being late. I consider lateness to be a cardinal sin. The ultimate disrespect."

"It's a good thing we're not actually running late, then." She opens the door and steps out.

Staring at her, my jaw nearly hits the floor.

She starts walking towards the door, only to stop and turn towards me. "Coming?"

I shake myself out of my amazed stupor. I would run hours late if it meant waiting for this creature to be ready. I hardly know where to look first: the shining hair, arranged in curls on top of her head? The shimmering dress which looks as though it were made of liquid silver? It flows over her body, and constantly in motion, drawing the eye no matter how she moves. It shows off her ample cleavage and long, toned legs without being too much. I find that sexier than anything else, the fact that something is left to the imagination. I stride over to her and she slips her hand through the crook of my elbow. We walk together to the elevator. I lean forward and hit the button.

"How do I look?" she asks, biting down on her crimson bottom lip.

Fuck, I want to take her lip between my teeth and bite down until she hisses. I swallow hard before speaking. Even so, my voice shakes. "You look…ravishing." It's the simplest and the most honest way to describe her.

She blushes. "I've never been called that before."

"You've never been with the right man before, then." And that's obvious. If Luke is any indication… "You should be reminded on a daily basis of how beautiful you are. How fortunate any man is to even be near you. You're so fucking beautiful."

"Now you're embarrassing me."

But the way her eyes shine tells me she likes it. She just isn't used to it. She'll just have to get used to it because I plan on complimenting her every day of our life together. I plan to rain compliments down on her until the only voice she hears in her head when she considers her looks is mine, telling her she's the most glorious creature to ever walk the earth.

"I don't mean to embarrass you," I assure her. "You deserve to know how stunning you look right now. After all, you did ask."

She grins. "That's true. I did."

"What's more important is how you feel. How does all of this make you feel?"

She can see herself in the reflection off the elevator doors.

I watch as a shy smile spreads across her face.

"I feel…pretty. No, more than that. I've felt pretty before, but this is different. I feel like another person."

"A little more powerful, maybe?" I suggest.

"Yes."

"And sexy?"

She turns her face away but agrees, "Yes."

I catch her chin in my fingers. Her skin feels like silk. I long to run my fingers down that long throat. And I will. Soon. Very soon. I smile at her. "That's good. You don't have to be embarrassed by that. You deserve to feel that way, because you are sexy. Men will fall at your feet tonight. I promise." And I'll want to kill every single one of them for even looking at her. This is going to be a difficult evening where I'll have to toe the line between pretending to be the affectionate fiancé to the rest of the world while giving Dani the impression that I see nothing growing between us.

"Will they?" she whispers.

The doors open, but neither of us move. Instead, we stare at each other, her eyes wide and heartbreakingly beautiful.

She places a trembling hand on my chest. "Will they really fall at my feet?"

Blood surges to my cock and it's only by supreme force of will that I don't haul her over my shoulder, carry her back to my bed, and fuck her all night long. But that would ruin everything, of course, and even I will admit she was right to end things the way she did, out on the balcony. At that time, I didn't feel so charitable about it, but I see now that it was the right move. I don't do stolen nights…I want it all.

Instead of pulling her to me and letting my hands explore her luscious body, I pat the back of her hand. "Yes. They will. And I'm going to have to keep a close eye on you because of it."

She takes my rejection like a champ, merely grinning as we make our way into the elevator. "Oh, great. I can hardly wait to have you trailing me around all night, punching any guy who dares speak a word to me."

"I won't have to trail around after you."

"Oh? Why not?"

"Because I plan to have you like this all night." I wrap an arm around her waist and hold her close to me. "No more distance than this. Right here."

"That might make it a little difficult to eat," she points out, her delicious tits pressed so sweetly against my abs.

"I'm sure we'll think of something." She's too tempting, looking up at me with her luscious lips parted just so, and her breath coming shallow and fast. I can't help myself, I bend my head and brush my lips against hers. Her sweet sigh gets me rock hard, and I very nearly lose my head. Thank God, then for Mark.

"Well. I can see now that I'll be on my own for most of the night," his voice announces from just outside the elevator.

I turn to see him smirking like the know-it-all he is.

CHAPTER 25

Brock

Mark manages to stop being smug long enough to flash a smile at my fake fiancée. I can tell from the warmth in his voice that he's impressed with her. And from the irritating way his eyes linger on her tits. Only when I clear my throat sternly does he bring his focus back to her face.

"Dani, this is Mark."

"Mark. Of course." She looks up at me with wide eyes. "Should you really be saying things like that out in the open?"

"What?"

"Introducing us like we've never met before," she whispers, reminding me for all the world of a little girl trying to keep a secret from her daddy. Endearing as hell.

"It makes sense that you wouldn't have met, since he's on the west coast now." I slide an arm around her waist because I just can't help but touch her when she flashes those wide, innocent eyes at me.

"She's smarter than you, brother." Mark punches my shoulder. "Though the bar isn't set all that high in the first place. No offense," he adds, grinning conspiratorially at Dani.

She laughs, and I can't help but note how instantly they have established some kind of rapport. I get the feeling they'll be good friends one day. A stark difference from Mark's uneasy, jealous-riddled relationship with Charlotte, which is what makes it so pathetically laughable that she would pretend he is her close friend after our break-up.

My best friend and Dani's easy laughter is what I hear as we walk into the banquet room. It feels like further proof that my relationship with Dani is the real thing. It doesn't matter that the huge room is chock-full of people I'd normally cross the road to avoid. Or that at some point during this evening, someone will come up and bore me to death. I'm flying high, I have the world on my arm, and she's laughing up at me with that beautiful face of hers.

And Charlotte can't stand it. She rushes over to us with a brilliant smile.

God, I've seen that smile so many times. That I'm-pretending-to-be-exuberant-so-you'll-be-jealous smile. Does she have any idea how obvious she is? Probably not, since that would require some measure of self-awareness, which she doesn't possess.

"Now the party can really start!" she bubbles, wrapping both arms around one of Mark's. "Wow. This is just like old times, isn't it?"

"How so?" I ask, raising an eyebrow and pulling Dani a little closer.

"Oh, you know. The three of us, together again." She gives Mark a little squeeze.

To his credit, he's not laughing too hard. Yet. "Yes, whenever I think of us, the Three Musketeers come to mind," he jokes. "And on that note, I need a drink. A stiff one."

"Open bar," she reminds us, her smile only faltering in the slightest when her eyes graze Dani's response by wriggling against me.

Fuck, she has no idea how potent she is. It's too much even for Charlotte. She mutters something about needing to talk to somebody and disappears into the crowd.

"I think we could all use a drink," I announce.

Dani nods. Her jaw is clenched tight. She's obviously not aware how deep under Charlotte's skin she's already gotten. But knowing her, she would never see herself in Charlotte's league and wouldn't believe it, and just change the subject.

"Jack and ginger. Make it two," I request from the bartender.

Dani looks surprised.

"You'll like it. Trust me. If you don't, by all means, toss it, but you look like you need something strong."

"Does it show?" She laughs shakily.

I respond by pulling her into me to the point where our bodies touch in too many places. She's so warm, sweet, and supple. She trembles a little, which only makes my blood pump harder. Faster. Until I can't hear anything but the pounding in my ears.

When I lean in, I brush my lips against her ear and can feel the shiver running through her. Holy shit, this is testing the limits of my control in ways nothing else ever has. "Remember what I said. How gorgeous you are. How you deserve to feel sexy." My arm tightens around her waist in a vice. "And how I plan to keep you this close all night. Because tonight, you're mine."

Her eyes widen and her mouth opens in a soft gasp.

I smile slowly. She's not quite as immune to me as she makes out.

CHAPTER 26

Dani

What is he doing to me? Driving me crazy, that's what.

It's not even fair. How can I keep separating what he's saying and doing, and what we're actually in this for? Because he is too darn convincing and it's getting harder and harder for me to not get my heart involved. I sort of want to remind him that he doesn't have to try so hard to make us look believable, but I also want to crawl into his lap and stay there.

It's complicated.

Real complicated.

Ugh…I wish he wasn't so darn right about the drink too. It's exactly what I need. Why does he have to be right about everything, always? If he were wrong every once in a while, it would make him seem a little more human, a little less perfect. To date, the only thing that makes him even the slightest bit relatable is the way he's still hung up on his ex. Strange considering she happens to be the most dreadful harpy I've ever met.

I look up at him from under my lashes. He's saying something to Mark. Is that creature really the kind of woman he goes for? I wish I could get Mark alone for a few minutes and ask him. He seems like a good guy. Fun, charming, playful with gently tanned skin. And he looks like a west coaster too, with his blond hair and piercing eyes. Almost as handsome as Brock, but in a different way.

My eyes look for and find Charlotte as she weaves her way through the crowd of guests, dragging Trent behind her and laughing that shrill laugh of hers. If I didn't know better, I'd think he was on his way to the dentist for a root canal tomorrow night, instead of getting married to the woman he loves. I guess that's the way marriage goes for people like him and her. They run in the same circles and have to marry within the circle or they'll feel as if they've married beneath them. Nevermind, they have nothing in common with each other as people or they're not hot for each other.

I turn my attention back to Brock. He's nodding and there is so much intelligence in his face. Could he really be in love with her? It seems almost unbelievable. He seems too smart and sophisticated not to be able to see through her act. I mean he saw right through me on our first meeting. Maybe she's really incredible in bed or something? Is that his Achilles heel? But are men really that stupid? Does sex blind them so much that they can't recognize a twenty-four-carat bitch when she shimmies up to them and treats them like a piece of shit?

"Catch you later," Brock says to Mark and turns to me. "What are you thinking about?" he asks, touching my bare shoulder.

I feel almost naked in this dress, no matter how sexy it is or how far his eyes popped out of his head when he first saw me in it, I'm not used to baring this much skin. "About how unreal this is," I lie with a shaky laugh. "This time last week, I was cleaning apartments and planning to do the same thing for the foreseeable future. But here I am. In this fine hotel, this high society party, in this wildly expensive designer dress...with you."

"Life can turn on a dime," he agrees.

"I'm still not entirely sure why you have me here with you," I confess. It must be the liquor loosening my tongue. I have to remember to take it easy, no matter how tasty it is. Drinking isn't my forte. I lose my tight control very fast and the last thing I need is to get drunk and make a big mistake.

"What do you mean?"

I shrug. "I don't think Charlotte believes you would be with someone like me."

"Trust me, I didn't make a mistake. You're so perfect you've got Charlotte dying to scratch your eyes out." He allows his fingers to trail down my arm, raising goosebumps.

I wish I could lean against him, absorb his touch, and ask him to take me upstairs. Oh, I want nothing more than to do that. There's an almost discernable pain in my chest I want it so much. "But what difference does it make? It's obvious she's miserable with this guy." I have to lean in close and murmur in his ear to be heard without giving us away, but it's not exactly a hardship. His cologne alone is enough to make my inner thighs tingle.

"You think so?" he replies, his voice deep and resonant, stirring the hairs on the back of my neck until they stand up.

Does he have any idea what he's doing to me?

"You don't see it?" I straighten and scan the room for her. I find her fast. It's hard to miss her in her skin-tight white dress. Like we need the reminder that she's the bride. The smile plastered on her face looks about as real as her hair extensions—admittedly, they're pretty high-quality, but they're clearly not the real deal. Nobody has hair like that, so thick and wild. That tamed-yet-untamed look. Actually, everything about her is a fake.

"You think she's pining away with love for me?"

I turn back to look at him. One corner of his sensuous lips curls upwards. I would if I were in her Jimmy Choos. Then again, I wouldn't let him get away from me in the first place. I stare up into his beautiful eyes. Again, I have a sensation of déjà vu. Which is really weird.

One eyebrow arches. He's waiting for my answer.

Gosh, I wish I didn't feel like this. I wish standing so close to him with his hand on my back and the scent of his cologne playing on my senses, didn't turn me into such a fool. I wish I could be stronger than I am, but I don't think I can. I'm only human, and he's—him. The most irresistible man I ever laid eyes on.

I clear my throat. "If she has half a brain in her head, she should," I say. It has to be the drink. I would never say something like that if I were sober.

"Dance with me."

"What?" Of all the ways he could respond, that was the last one I would've expected. The music is light, a sort of nondescript, inoffensive dance tune, and a few couples are already taking a turn on the floor.

"Let's dance. Isn't that what people who are in love do?"

I blink at him. *Oh, God. In love?* "Um…"

"Come on. You can show me some of your dance moves." He takes my hand and leads me across the room.

I don't dare protest or make a scene. Besides, the thought of having an excuse to be so close to him is exciting. When we reach the dance floor and he turns to pull me into an embrace, I stand on tiptoe to speak into his ear, "Exactly how much do we have to play this up?"

His eyes flash when they meet mine, and the closest thing to an electrical current I can imagine runs up my spine. I'm his. He doesn't know it. He can never know it. I even wish it weren't true, because there's no way this will end well. In spite of that, I would do anything he asked right now. Absolutely anything.

"Let me show you," he answers, and lets his body do all the talking as he holds me tight, pressing his hand into my lower back and forcing our bodies together. I wind my arms around his neck to support myself and let him lead me as we begin swaying back and forth, our hips rocking in time.

He lowers his head until his mouth skims over my shoulder,

then up my throat. The pressure from his lips is so slight, it might just as well not be there at all. Maybe I'm imagining it because that's what I wish he would do. I wish he would kiss me. And not just for show, the way he is now. I tilt my head back to get a look at him and one corner of his mouth quirks up in a sexy smirk.

Daring me? Maybe.

I press my face to the side of his neck when his hand slides down my back and just barely grazes the top of my butt. We never agreed to anything like this but it's all so good, so right. I wouldn't stop him for anything in the world. I can feel his pulse throbbing in his neck, just under my lips, and I want to sweep my tongue over that spot.

The urge to do so is almost impossible to fight, especially with the buzzing, tingling feeling between my legs getting stronger every time our bodies rub against each other. I'm breathless, dizzy, holding on for dear life now, as he controls our motion. A bead of sweat rolls down his neck and disappears under his shirt collar and oh, God—I want to lick it off. I have to squeeze my eyes shut to block it out.

But there's no blocking out the touch of his hands on me, my dress sliding over my skin until I'm so completely lost in sensation I don't ever want to be found. When I dare open my eyes again, he's looking down at me and our mouths are only inches from each other as we're both breathing hard and heavy— oh, yes, I'm lost. Falling. Wanting to fall even further...

The song is over. So is our dance. He steps back, breaking the spell. Probably for the best.

I need another drink. He takes my hand and we walk

towards the bar where he gets us a drink. I drink mine like it is water.

Brock's eyes widen.

"Can I have another?"

Without a word, he turns to orders another one.

I look around and to my surprise, my gaze gets entangled by Charlotte. We stare at each other. I just can't look away from the hate in her eyes. Then someone calls to her and she tears her eyes away from mine.

Wow! What the hell?

"Are you all right?" Brock asks, handing me my drink.

I can feel the heat from the alcohol and the sexual tension throbbing in my veins. Screw it! I'll give her something to be really jealous about. I take his hand and pull him towards the gardens. Outside the night is balmy. I run my hand over the nape of my neck. It is already damp.

"So…what are we doing out here, Dani?" Brock's voice is soft, his huge hand on my waist.

God, what would it be like to be on my back in his bed? I squeeze my thighs together as I remember how thick and long his erection was pressed into my belly. It's enough to soak my panties. I'm on fire—for the taste of Brock.

I turn around to face him. I don't know what I'm doing. I just feel this crazy heat inside me, between my legs. I know I shouldn't, but hell—this is Vegas. "Let's pretend to make out in that shed there."

His eyebrows almost disappear into his hairline.

No, I'm not the sane Dani I've known all my life. This Dani is fierce and powerful and knows exactly how to get what she wants. I'll give him something to remember me for when he thinks he still wants her. I tell myself this, but I know it's a lie. I want this for myself. This is for me to remember for when this weekend is over.

CHAPTER 27

Brock

I let her drag me to the little shed where children play in the daytime. She pushes open the yellow and blue door then bending her head, she enters. I follow her willingly. Inside, it's no bigger than a sauna room and almost as hot. It is lit only by the light filtering in through the two little windows. There's mud on the floor. Basically, it's hot and dirty, and fucking perfect.

I'm as horny as fuck. I've never felt this kind of raw lust before.

There is a bench along one wall. She pushes me towards it and kneels in front of me. Moisture pools under my arms, and a bead of sweat rolls down my back. Never in my wildest dreams did I imagine we would be back in a schoolyard scenario. I stare at her in amazement. Her pupils are dilated and her skin glistens with sweat. The smell of her perfume mingles with the smell of earth and makes her seem darkly sensual. She has no notion of how incredibly sexy she looks crouched between my legs.

My cock is so hard the ache almost makes me double over. "What do you want?" I ask her.

Her little tongue comes out and licks at her lips. "I want to suck you."

Shit, I've never been so turned on by a woman saying that to me. Keeping eye contact with her, I undo my belt and trousers.

When I free my cock, her gaze slides down. Her breath catches when she sees my dick. She licks her lips again. As if she can't wait to taste it. "Oh, my," she whispers.

"Yeah."

She brushes her fingers along my jaw and rests them on my lips.

I love the sensation of her soft skin. I curl my tongue around her fingers and suck them into my mouth. Her skin smells clean and fresh.

She watches me, mesmerized. Then she leans into me and lets her forehead touch mine. Her fingers slip out of my mouth. Her lips touch mine as I pull her to me and wrap my strength around her. My kiss is bruising and my tongue unapologetic, as it thrusts into her mouth.

She tastes of whiskey, ginger and something that is uniquely her. The taste of her drives me wild. Enveloped in my heat, she surrenders her mouth beautifully, welcoming my savagery. She's mine and I want all of her. I savor the sense of power I get from her total submission.

I'm addicted to her. I know that now.

I hold her in place while my palms skim her curves. She moans into my mouth and I squeeze her hips. She slides her palms over my shirt and I deepen the kiss even more. My lips roam along her smooth jaw before dipping down to her throat. I can't help it. My teeth clamp down on the base of her neck. She whimpers and a bolt of energy shoots to my cock. I know I wanted to take it easy with her, but fuck...

I pull away from her.

She's panting and her eyes are burning with need.

With a groan, I touch her face. Her skin feels hot and satiny. "Do you have any idea what you are doing to me?'

"No, but I want to make you moan my name," she whispers.

She is unbelievable.

I pull down the zipper of her dress and push aside the material. It is one of those dresses with an inbuilt bra. Her ripe full breasts spill out. Oh, fuck! I dip my head and take one rosy nipple between my lips. I suck it hard and her hips buck restlessly.

"Oh Brock," she groans, her chest heaving. Her head drops back exposing her creamy throat and breasts to me. I growl at the sight. With the last grip on my sanity gone, I lose track of everything but the swollen nipple in my mouth. Clinging to me, she moans sweetly as I carry on sucking. With my eyes, my fingers, my tongue and my body I tell her that she is mine. That I will explore her body to my heart's content.

I suck on her neck and she lets me. We both know there will be a mark there tomorrow to tell everyone that she is mine.

She pulls away suddenly and dips her head down. Using both her hands, she clasps the base of my cock firmly. I feel her hot breath before the silky wetness of her mouth envelops me. I revel in the warmth and sweetness of her mouth, as she eases the head of my cock between her plump lips, and slides her tongue along my burning skin making me cry out. When she sucks my dick all the way in it bumps the back of her throat, she eases up a little to keep from gagging. But Goddamn, she dives right back down.

I'm never letting her go anywhere again. She is mine now.

"Yes. Right there, baby," I encourage.

She sinks down further than before, until I feel my cock head stroke her throat. She pulls up again, and I feel her relax her muscles before she glides down again. She gets a little further down.

I savor every second, every sensation.

I know she's not going to get all of me in, but damn I love that she is trying so hard. Still sucking my shaft, she cups my balls in one hand, rolling and firmly stroking them. My heart is pounding and my cock pulses hard. I'm dying to come, but I don't want this to be over yet. Hell, not ever.

My hips buck, and she lets me thrust into her mouth and throat. Her eyes roll up to find me watching as I fuck her mouth.

Whoa. I lose it then. I can't take anymore.

"I'm gonna come…" I warn, so she can remove her mouth if she doesn't want me to come in it.

Looking up at me she carries on sucking, up and down the length of me. She wants me to come in her mouth. The knowledge wipes out the last of my control. I rear back and she sinks down one last time, taking me deep inside her throat.

Roaring her name, I reach out and pinch her swollen nipples as the first spurts of my cum coat her tongue. While I shoot the rest of my release, her eyes never leave me. My thrusts slow, then still, and she swallows it all, every last drop. I marvel at how beautiful she looks with my cock buried in her face. I never want this moment to end.

She carries on sucking gently.

God, I love this woman.

I reach out to gently stroke her cheek. It gleams with a sheen of sweat. "Now it's your turn. But we're not doing it here."

I withdraw my cock from her mouth and zip myself back in. Then I help her dress.

CHAPTER 28

Dani

I bend my head and come out of the children's playhouse. I think I'm in shock. I have never done anything like that before. But something about Brock just makes me do these crazy things. Ever since I met him, I've been doing all these weird things that are totally unlike me. Now, all I can think of is getting to our suite and having my turn. Letting those big hands of his spread me open and taking that massive cock deep inside me.

He appears next to me, his face flushed and his eyes glittering.

I bite my lip. "Do we look like we...did it?"

He doesn't laugh. "Why should we? We haven't done it yet."

We walk quickly hand in hand through the grassy area and enter the huge room once again. The party is in full swing.

As we are about to exit the room, Charlotte calls to us, "Hey, wait up."

Both of us stop and turn around.

She comes up to us laughing. "Where do you two think you're escaping to?"

"I have a headache. I'm just going upstairs to lie down for a bit." See what I mean about me doing all kinds of crazy things ever since I met Brock. I'm not a fan of liars, but that lie just tripped off my tongue.

She rearranges her face into one of empathy and pity. The fake bitch. "Oh no, I'm so sorry. You're going to miss a great party."

"Yeah, I guess, I will. Sorry."

"Nevermind." She grabs my wrist. "At least have a chocolate before you go. They've been specially flown in from Paris just for our engagement. I swear, it would have been cheaper to give out gold to our guests." She smiles and holds out a box. "Aren't they gorgeous?"

The chocolates do look very fancy with an entwined C and T on them.

"Go on, take one," she urges.

I pick one and pop it into my mouth. It's good. Very good. The truffle center melts on my tongue.

She offers the tray to Brock.

He shakes his head. "Thanks, but I'm not in the mood for chocolate right now. I better get Dani back to bed. Don't want her headache to get any worse."

"All right then. Run along both of you. See you both tomorrow. Good night."

I turn to Brock, surprised. "That was very civil of her."

"Yes, I thought so too." He presses the button on the elevator panel and turns to me. "Jesus, I can't wait to get you back to our suite."

With a smile, I get into the elevator. Two women come in behind us. They get off at the second floor. I smile wickedly at Brock and he slides his arm around my back. I look up into his blue, blue eyes as his head starts to descent.

At that moment, I feel an itch on my on the inside of my knee. "Hang on," I whisper and bend to scratch it. I lift my head and the area feels hot and itchy again. For a second, I think I must have stepped on some poison Ivy or something in the garden, and then I feel an itch on my stomach and I know. *Oh, shit.*

"What's the matter?" Brocks asks with a frown.

"Strawberries. I've eaten strawberries."

"How?" he asks, horrified.

I don't even have to think. "It must have been the chocolates."

"What?"

"Charlotte must have swiped the chocolates with a piece of strawberry or something."

Fury replaces the lust I've seen all evening in his eyes. "Do you have the necessary medication?" he asks urgently.

"No, I didn't bring my antihistamines."

"Damn that bitch," he swears under his breath.

"It might not be her."

"Of course, it's her," he says, his jaw clenched tight.

"Well, we can't prove it anyway."

The doors open. He lets us into our suite.

By now, I am full on scratching at my skin. He rushes to the phone and orders a doctor to come immediately, and asks him to bring an allergy kit with him.

For the next twenty minutes I clench my hands into fists to stop myself from scratching, and Brock paces the floor like a caged panther until the doctor arrives. He gives me a injection and makes me better almost immediately, but by then neither of us are in the mood.

I just feel tired and grubby and Brock is just tight-lipped with fury. I say goodnight and close my bedroom door.

After a cool shower, I turn up the air-conditioning. Cold air always helps. My skin is full of red patches. I apply the soothing aloe vera gel to all the angry red patches on my body. By tomorrow, I know I will be fine again.

Then I go to stand at the window and look down.

The strip is so beautiful. Sparkling. I wonder how many people are down there, wagering everything they have. Or just living it up, having the time of their lives. Or getting married. So many people with their stories and the things that matter to them.

And me, watching from my window. Alone in my room. My extremely extravagant, elegant, comfortable room. Like nothing I've ever experienced. I feel like a queen up here, looking down on my subjects while wrapped in the plush bathrobe included with the suite.

How many people have worn this robe? And were they as mixed-up as I am?

There were no more dances after that first one, which is a good thing. Maybe instead of being angry with Charlotte I should be grateful. Maybe it is better this way. I drank too much alcohol and it went to my head. It's a good thing I didn't sleep with him.

My mind starts playing out the evening. Going back over all the crazy minutes, the looks, the little touches and caresses, what we did in the children's playhouse. It's almost enough to make me angry with myself.

"Cut it out," I hiss, shaking my head.

As I stand there shivering in the cold air, one thing is clear. I'm only making things harder for myself. It's easy for him. It's all a sham, a game, and nothing more. Sure, he'll have to get over Charlotte. I can't imagine that taking much longer, especially once she's married and he's seen it happen with his own two eyes and that's the end of that.

I, on the other hand, will have to nurse this lust or whatever it is for a long time. The memories of his hands on me, his cock in my mouth, will pop up at the worst moments. Like tonight, while I'm trying to sleep.

While he sleeps in his own room, nursing a heartache of his own.

For Charlotte.

CHAPTER 29

Dani

I f he's heartbroken, he's hiding it well. After checking that there is no lasting damage from last night's strawberry fiasco, Brock is all sunshine and smiles.

"Come on. Mark tells me the slots pay out like crazy," Brock says as we leave the suite, full of energy.

"You clearly slept well last night," I observe with a wry grin.

"Like a baby," he confirms. "You?"

"I wish I could say the same." The last time I checked the clock, it was after five. No matter how long I waited with my eyes closed, I couldn't fall asleep. Not with Brock's face swimming around in my head, not with the scent of him still alive in my memory.

He frowns deeply. "I thought you said you were okay?"

"I am. It wasn't anything to do with the allergy. I guess I'm just not used to drinking."

"You only had three."

"Which is two more than I'm used to having before going to bed." I shrug. I wish he would let it go. I should've told him I never slept so well in my entire life. He doesn't need to know the truth.

"I'll keep that in mind from now on. You don't sleep well after having a few drinks."

I look up at him as we walk through the courtyard which leads to the adjoining casino. "You won't have to keep it in mind for much longer."

"Careful when you say things like that," he warns. "We're engaged, remember?"

"Of course, of course." I roll my eyes when he's not looking. It's impossible not to get a little annoyed with him when he says things like that. I'm glad he still thinks this is all a game, but it isn't for me. That's not his fault, but I can't help the way I feel either. I need to keep in mind that I'm doing this for the money.

"Are you all right?" he asks, like he just read my mind.

Or my face. I know it's pretty expressive. I can't count all the times I've gotten into trouble after letting my true thoughts shine through on my face. "Yeah, I'm fine." I force a smile. "Do you gamble a lot?"

"No. Do you?"

"I've never gambled before."

"You've never gambled? Not even a lotto ticket?" he teases.

"No." I laugh. "I haven't even been legally allowed to gamble for very long, you know."

"Aww... my baby." He winks, and takes my hand as we enter the casino.

I blink hard, looking around, taking it all in at once. I don't know what I expected. Something louder, I guess. Smoky. Seedy. Nothing like what I see in front of me now.

"It's actually quite beautiful," I whisper, instantly embarrassed at what a nerd I must sound like. Who says something like that? But it's the truth. A giant, blown glass chandelier hangs in the center of the room, shining down on the chrome slot machines and their blinking lights. There are banks of them just about everywhere, along with tables with all sorts of games. I only recognize a few of them. I should've done a little research last night, instead of wasting all that time trying to sleep.

Brock doesn't look as though he thinks I'm a nerd. He looks thrilled, in fact, his eyes are shining like the ocean on a bright sunny day again, as he leads me further into the casino. "Come on. Let's have a little fun."

"What do you want to do?" I ask, my head swiveling back and forth. There are so many people here, all at once. It's not even noon, but here they are. And I'm one of them. I never dreamed I would spend this weekend in a place like this. What an adventure this has turned out to be.

"Oh, so many things..." he mutters cynically, and just loud enough for me to hear.

I don't think I was supposed to hear it, honestly, but I did.

And my palms instantly start to sweat. "Why don't you pick something we could do here, in the casino?" I suggest with a giggle.

"Since you insist." He scans the room. "We can start on the slots. I'll take it slow, and be gentle with you. Since you're a virgin."

"Shut up!" I squeal, slapping his shoulder with my palm.

He grabs my wrist and holds it behind my back and pushes himself right up against me. "Hey. No shame. We all start off as virgins, right?"

I stare at his mouth as it curves up in a knowing smile. This man is sex on a stick. Why does he have to be so sexy? "Don't be a jerk," I croak.

He lets me go with a smirk, and turns toward a bank of machines.

I'm almost relieved for the distraction. My knees are a little weak, and there goes the tingling between my legs again. Stronger than last night, even. I pick a machine at random and sit.

He slips a hundred dollar bill into the machine and I start to play...and darned if this isn't the most fun I've had in forever. How in the world is this so much fun? "All I'm doing is pulling on this arm over and over. Why is it so addictive?"

He chuckles as he leans in over my shoulder, while his hand closes over the one I've wrapped around the machine's arm. "If you think it's fun to pull on this..."

"Oh, come on!" I laugh, elbowing him even as my heart skips

a beat. "Sorry, but unless you're going to open your mouth and spew out a fortune…"

"I thought I already had," he murmurs.

I give him my best withering look. "Is that what you think I think of you? That you're just a slot machine?"

"No. At least, I hope not. And if you do, I'm more than willing to prove otherwise."

"You don't need to prove anything. I hope you know me well enough by now to know I would never think that about anybody, especially not you."

He sits on the stool next to mine, leaning forward with his elbows on his knees until only inches of air separates us. "Maybe I want to prove to you that I'm more than that."

I must be imagining this. I'm back up in the suite, finally sleeping, dreaming the most vivid dream of my life. But the sound of bells and cheers are real, just like the goosebumps running up and down my arms. I can't be dreaming them. "And how would you go about doing that?" I ask in a voice that shakes and gives away my nerves.

"I'm sure I could think of something."

"I bet you could." I reach for the arm of the slot machine just to have something to do, and pull down. We both jump in surprise when a siren sounds.

"What?" I scream.

"You won," he says, laughing.

"I won?"

He nods.

"I won!" I scream, jumping up and down, clapping hard enough that my hands hurt.

Brock picks me up and swings me around in a circle, his laughter ringing in my ears as the machine's screen lights up with, WINNER!

I'm almost excited enough to not notice the way his hands warm my skin even through the sundress between us.

Almost.

A casino employee issues a huge payout slip with my winnings, but Brock and I are too busy staring at each other to even look at it. Everything I told myself last night about protecting my heart just slips away. I don't even know how much the machine paid out. It sort of doesn't matter at that moment. There are more important things to focus on. Like the way Brock's hands linger on my back. The way my breasts are pressed up against his chest. And the way it feels like something is choking me and I can't quite breathe because of that look in his eyes.

Something is going to happen, and I'm not going to stop it. I want it too badly.

When he takes me by the hand and leads me from the casino, I follow without a word.

CHAPTER 30

Dani

T he doors of the elevator swish close. We are alone. The wall of the elevator car is hard, unforgiving, when Brock pushes me against it. His eyes bore holes into me, staring into my soul. When he speaks, his voice is raspy with desire, "I didn't sleep all night thinking about you."

My jaw drops. "Really?"

"Yes, really," he mocks. Sinking his hands into my hair, he pulls my face to his, crushing our mouths together.

It's so much better than it was before because it's for us—just us. He thrusts his hips, grinding against me, the pressure from his hardening dick a reminder of what's about to happen. I return the pressure and his groan sends shivers all through me.

He wants me. He wants this.

So do I. Oh, Lord—so do I. I can't help but wrap a leg around his thigh, pulling him even closer as his kiss leaves me panting. The doors can't open soon enough. When they do, he lifts me to waist-height and I wrap my legs around him, with his mouth still covering mine. We burst through the door to the suite and he doesn't take me to the bedroom. Instead, he pushes me against the closed door, and holds me there with the weight of his body.

"God, you drive me crazy," he groans, his hands now free to slide over my skin.

I lean my head against the door, moaning his name while his mouth skims my throat and his tongue darts out, hot and hungry. "Jesus, Dani," he rasps, his fingers digging into my thigh before moving further up my leg.

My cries echo through the suite as he caresses the curve of my butt, teasing both of us. He's right at the lacy hem of my damp panties, stroking the sensitive skin, and my fingers turn into claws as I clutch his shoulders.

"Oh, my God," I moan as his mouth moves lower, lower. His tongue slides between my breasts and laps at my cleavage. I hold his head close, urging him on, whispering his name over and over, while he grunts like an animal and grinds his rock-hard bulge against my belly. His fingers dip down there, between my thighs, and he groans louder than ever when he feels how wet I am.

And now...he's on his knees and sliding my panties down. My head rolls from side to side when he buries his face between my legs. God, I'm in heaven. Fireworks explode behind my eyelids as I writhe in ecstasy. His tongue sweeps up and down the length of my slit, lapping up my juices.

"You taste so sweet…" he moans before going deeper.

When the tip of his tongue touches my aching, throbbing bundle of nerves, my thighs clench, and to my complete shock, an explosive orgasm rocks me to my core. I don't know whether he's laughing at how easy it was to get me off, or grunting with need as he continues to probe with his greedy tongue. All I know is, I'm floating in a haze of pleasure and I don't want to ever come back down to Earth.

He stands and sweeps me up in his arms. Carrying me to my room which is closer and places me on my bed. He peels off his shirt, revealing a body that looks like it was chiseled out of marble. Warm, tanned, glistening, tattooed marble. My hands ache to touch him. I need to feel his skin on mine. I sit up to unzip my dress and he works it over my head. Then his hands are gliding over my raised arms and down to my waist, and back up to where he unhooks my bra. "Your body…" he whispers as he takes my breasts in his hands. "Is unbelievable. I want to worship this body."

I drape my arms over his bare shoulders, pull him down on top of me, and relish the sensation of his hard, masculine body pressing into mine while we kiss and grind against each other. I never thought it could be like this, so exciting, so breathless and so, so hot. The tension in my core tightens with every kiss, every touch, every taste of his skin or soft moan. My hand brushes against his straining dick.

"I need you. Fuck, how I need you," he groans.

My fingers close around his length. So thick. I thought I was drunk and dreamed it last night, but no, it is extraordinarily thick. The cotton briefs he's wearing are still between us, and he practically tears them off. "I need you too," I whisper back.

I touch him while he searches his pants for a condom, taking him in with my eyes, hands and mouth when he comes into reach. He's undone me, fully and completely, and I'm not thinking rationally anymore. I'm only feeling and acting on what my body has wanted ever since I first opened my eyes to find him watching me sleep.

The pressure at my entrance is enough to make me grit my teeth. He's big, thicker than I've ever taken before, and I'm torn between anticipation and apprehension.

He kisses me softly, teasingly, and looks deep into my eyes as he pushes forward, watching my reaction as he slowly enters me inch by glorious inch, stretching me until I'm sure I can't take more.

But I do. I want all of him, and my body adjusts quickly.

He begins thrusting then—deep, sure thrusts. Again and again, until my eyes close and my mouth falls open to allow cries of lust to fill the room. I've never been loud like this before, but I can't be quiet. Not now. It's like I've been playing in the minor leagues before now, and I finally understand what it's all about.

True passion, true pleasure.

He falls onto his forearms, his weight heavy and welcome, and I wrap my legs around him to drive him further inside me. I want all of him, always. Forever. I know that isn't possible, but I can't help wishing this was for always. Gently, I lick away the sweat from his throat and listen as he whispers my name against my neck. It's all so sweet, so perfect. We work together, moving as one, until we both lose control and dissolve into frenzied bucking, crying out each time our bodies slam together.

"Yes!" I scream, clenching around him as I explode.

He follows close behind.

We hold each other there for a minute as we come back down and our quivering bodies are all that's left of our tremendous climaxes.

And the memories.

I'll always have the memories. A single tear trickles down my cheek, and I brush it away before he raises his head from my shoulder.

"Are you all right?" he asks apprehensively, brushing hair away from my face.

"The earth moved for me." I grin, trying to keep it light-hearted. "Or couldn't you tell?"

He smiles, relieved, and rolls away even though I want nothing more than to hold him forever. All I can do is try to put myself together and wonder where we're supposed to go from here.

Propping himself up on one elbow, he looks down at me tenderly. "You have no idea how much I've been wanting to do that."

I blush all over. "Really?"

"I wasn't just playing at flirting with you, you know."

"I thought we were—umm—pretending." My heart feels as if it's about to burst when he draws me into his arms. We're on the cusp of something amazing. I can just feel it.

His phone buzzes, startling both of us.

"Oh, for Christ's sake. It's okay. They're just texts."

"No, look at them. They may be important," I say softly.

He looks as if he is about to say something else, but then just sighs and reaches for his phone.

I have to extricate myself from his arms to allow him to do so. I sit up against the pillows. I watch as he reads his messages, his expression darkening.

He looks out the window for a moment, like he's weighing his options.

My heart sinks. "What is it?"

"It's Mark. He needs a little sanity. Apparently, the bride has been a terror all day. She's been screaming and cursing at the wedding party, and even threatened to back out of the entire event and go to the chapel in town. The wedding planner is in tears. He just made it out of the rehearsal."

"Imagine that," I say dryly.

"After the stunt she pulled last night, I don't care if I never see her again."

I shrug. "But it's not her who wants some moral support, is it?"

"Mark's a big boy. He can handle his own shit."

"It's okay. Go on. Be a good friend to him. We can catch up later."

He stares at me with an inscrutable expression. "You sure?"

"Absolutely," I say firmly.

"Do you know that you are incredible?"

"I do. But you are allowed to remind me occasionally."

Grinning, he sprints out of bed and goes to his room. He returns after having put on a black t-shirt and jeans, looking more casual than I've ever seen him. It's a good look. Then again, he could wear anything and look good.

"Buy him a drink for me, huh?" I grin, settling back against the pillows. I can handle him leaving me to help his best friend.

"What about you? Will you catch up on some sleep?" He sits on the edge of the bed, suddenly tender and intimate.

It feels like every dream I've ever had just came roaring to life. My insides feel all gooey. I make a mental note to pinch myself when he's out of the room. Just in case. "I don't think I have the time. I made an appointment at the salon. Gotta look my best tonight, right?"

His smile is sweet as he runs a strand of my hair through his fingers. "You look pretty damn good to me right now."

"I'm glad you think so, but I doubt this ensemble would be considered acceptable for a fancy Vegas wedding."

We both chuckle softly before he plants a passionate kiss on my waiting lips. My fingers claw into his hair.

He pulls back, his eyes dark. "Damn, but it is so hard to leave you."

I smile at it this. "Go on. I'll see you this evening?"

He kisses me again, and stands up. "Okay. Don't do anything I wouldn't."

"Ha, ha," I say.

He walks to the door and blows me a kiss.

I catch it. It feels so natural, normal. Like we could be an actual couple in another life, another world in which things like that actually happen to people like me.

Then again, maybe this is that world.

When Brock turns to throw me one last look before leaving —there's something in his eyes that wasn't there before. I sternly tell myself not to get carried away. It could be my imagination. Or a trick of the light.

CHAPTER 31

Dani

I kind of hope to run into Brock and Mark downstairs. Or just Brock. I wouldn't mind another kiss. If we were convincing before, I can just imagine how much more we'll be now.

The thought of it makes me smile, biting my lip in anticipation of what might happen. I don't want to believe this could ever go further than it already has, but my heart's already miles ahead of my brain. Nobody can make love the way he made love to me without feeling something, can they?

I'm so busy recalling what just happened upstairs and wondering what else we might do later, maybe after the wedding, that I don't notice Charlotte until she's practically standing on top of me.

And she's still in full-on Bridezilla mode. I'm surprised there aren't flames shooting from her eyes as she glares at me. "What are you doing down here by yourself?" she demands, like she's accusing me of a crime.

I look at her closely. She really has some balls. There's no remorse at all for what she did to me last night. Well, I won't give her the satisfaction of knowing I suffered last night. Let her think her plan didn't have any success. "What do you mean?" I ask with a friendly smile.

She rolls her eyes. "I mean, it isn't like Brock to let his woman wander around on her own."

"You make him sound like a caveman." I chuckle. What I really want to do is slap the smug look off her face, but a catfight in the middle of the lobby probably wouldn't bode well for the rest of the weekend. And something tells me nothing would make her happier than seeing me break down and lose my cool.

"Well? Isn't he? I mean, if he's serious about you, I would imagine he's got you on a pretty short leash." She eyes me up and down with a smirk, not even trying to fake niceness any more.

Truly, I like it this way. I always prefer to know exactly where I stand with a person. "Maybe he just trusts me," I suggest with a shrug.

Her eyes darken and narrow into thin slits. Yeah, that got her. But she's not just giving up and going away, she's just warming up. She leans in. "Or maybe he doesn't care enough to get jealous."

I'm quaking inside. She's right. He doesn't really care about me, and it's obvious to her because she knows him really. Even though I'm here to make her believe he loves me, I've fallen short. She's seen right through our lie. And it is still a lie. No amount of mind-blowing sex will change that. Darn her for doing this to me.

She folds her tanned, toned arms and smiles in smug triumph. "I knew it."

"Knew what?"

"He's still in love with me, but he's just too proud to admit it. That's why he came here this weekend. Because he can't stand knowing I'm marrying another man without being here to see it for himself. I wonder if he'll even be able to get through the ceremony without objecting."

I gaze at her in wonder. "You're deluded."

"We'll see," she whispers with a triumphant smile. Then she turns on her heel and walks away.

I wish I could sink into the floor and never come back. I don't think I've ever experienced this level of humiliation. No amount of money is worth this. I can't believe I ever agreed to leave myself open to this.

After all, who in their right mind would believe Brock would actually want me? I'm nothing compared to Charlotte. Maybe I'm smarter, and I'm a decent person, but what difference does that make in this cruel world? If he went for a girl like her, she's the kind of girl he really wants. Sexy, flashy, sophisticated. I was crazy to ever think a few hot kisses and an afternoon in bed can make any difference.

I stand in the middle of the foyer. I was going to the spa, wasn't I?

It all seems pointless now. Why would I bother looking as good as I can tonight when Brock doesn't really want me and Charlotte knows it? Then I straighten my shoulders. I took on this job and I will do it to the best of my ability. Brock will never be able to accuse me of doing half the job. Only sheer willpower keeps my feet moving in the right direction. I may have done a very, very stupid thing to get emotionally involved with Brock, but it doesn't mean I have to go to the wedding not looking my best.

I still have my pride.

"You seem rather tense this afternoon." The stylist frowns at me in the mirror, where I can gauge the progress she's making on my hair. It hangs in long curls, fresh out of the rollers she just removed.

"Oh, I'm fine," I lie through my teeth.

"Maybe you should spend a little time with the masseuse," she suggests. "If you clench your teeth any harder, you'll break them."

"Is it that obvious?" I ask, my shoulders slumping. A complete and total stranger sees how depressed I am right now. I'm sure Brock will be able to see it too, and that just makes me feel worse.

"I'm afraid it is," she confirms cheerfully.

Of course, she might just be trying to sell a massage. What do the masseuses do? Tell their clients they have split ends? It's a relief when my phone buzzes. Saved by the text.

And what a text. From Brock.

Where are you? Get up here now. We need to talk ASAP.

Oh, wonderful. I'm halfway through my appointment and he needs to talk. No, he demands to talk. Where does he get off demanding anything from me?

Oh, right. He's the person giving me a quarter of a million bucks for being here with him. I guess I could make something out of the way my hair currently looks. "I'm going to have to cut this short," I explain, removing my cape. At least, I don't have to answer any more questions about what's wrong with me.

Anyway, he needs to know about my little altercation with Charlotte. He should know that we didn't fool her. She might act like her bitchy, smug self when we see each other after the wedding and it will go better if he can anticipate what she thinks she knows. Or what she's absolutely right about.

That he's still in love with her.

God, why was I stupid enough to forget that part? I should've put a stop to what happened today. Still, I can't pretend I didn't want it just as much as he seemed to.

"Brock?" I call out when I open the door to the suite and find that he's not waiting for me. I expected to see him standing in living room, hands clasped behind his back, demanding to know why it took me so long to get upstairs. Instead, the suite is quiet.

"Hello?" I walk to his closed bedroom door and tap gently on it. What if this is the opposite of what I'm thinking? What if he brought me up here for Round Two? And what do I do if that's the case? I open the door. "Brock? You in here?"

He's not.

Charlotte is.

CHAPTER 32

Dani

Charlotte bolts upright in bed, gasping and clutching the sheets around her naked body.

I have to lean against the wall because—oh, my God, the room is spinning. This is a nightmare. I fell asleep in the elevator, or down at the spa and this is just the worst nightmare of my entire life.

It has to be.

I open my mouth, but nothing comes out. I try again. "What are you doing here?" As though I need an explanation. I can't understand this. Because having sex with only one woman in a single afternoon isn't enough for him, I guess. His side of the bed looks messed up and the shower is running.

"What's it look like?" Charlotte challenges, glaring at me like she has the right to be annoyed that I'm here.

I tremble for a moment before coming back to my senses. Well, I won't let her make me feel like the bitch here. "It looks like you slept with Brock on *your* wedding day, you slut." I've never, ever in my entire life, said something like that to someone. Not to their face, at any rate, but she truly deserves it.

The bathroom door opens before she has the chance to reply, and I turn my rage towards Brock.

He steps into the room wearing a towel around his waist and nothing else.

Rage and heartbreak. How could he do this? All the things he said. And he had to go and sleep with her now, after having sex with me this morning.

God, I was so stupid.

We stare at each other in shock. I suppose if I'm honest it's not like he lied to me, is it? He told me he was still in love with his ex and wanted to make her jealous. He told me this was a business arrangement, and I wanted it that way. And maybe it has worked out perfectly for him. I made her jealous. She came to him and now, they are together. Maybe I have no right to suffer through the chest-crushing heartache at the sight of his face, but here I am. Suffering nonetheless.

"What the fuck?" he says.

"You pig! How could you do something like this? How could either of you?" I yell. I don't stick around to wait for his pathetic excuses, since I have no desire to hear any of them. I wish I could forget all of this, forget I ever met him. Forget the way he touched me and kissed me and stared into my eyes...

"Wait, Dani!"

He's probably following me, but I don't care. I can't stop. I don't ever want to see him again. If I look into those eyes, I might want to believe the lies he'll inevitably spew and I can't leave myself open to him. Not anymore. Not when he'd go so far as to have sex with her. Her! The same day as me, hours before her wedding. I never really knew him. He must be as cunning and manipulative as she is. No wonder he wants her. They're perfect for each other. The thought bounces through my head as I run through the suite and back through the door, out into the hallway.

I can still hear him as I throw myself into the elevator, calling my name. Let him. He got what he wanted, didn't he? He got his real, big true love back. I was just the cleaner that he paid to do a job. My eyes fill with tears of self-pity. I dash them away.

No, I should take responsibility for my pain. It's not his fault I was stupid enough to give my heart to someone who never lied about who they were truly in love with. By the time the doors glide open to reveal the lobby, I'm half-blinded by tears and choked by sobs. I don't even know where I'm going or how I'll get there. I left everything upstairs. I just want to go back home to my little apartment and my little job. At least there, I knew where I stood. I was the cleaner. I cleaned their shit and they paid me money. They didn't pretend to want me and hurt me. I've never felt this lost in my life.

"Dani?" Mark takes me by the shoulders when I bump into him. Literally. I can hardly see a thing and don't care very much, anyway.

At least, I bumped into someone familiar.

"What's wrong?"

"I—I can't talk about it," I babble, shaking my head. I have to get away from him too. He belongs to the same class of people. People who use their money and everyone around them to get whatever they want. Anyway, the last thing I want is to talk about Brock with his best friend. I don't want to talk to anybody about what just happened.

It's all too shameful.

He seems to understand this. At least, the slight smile he gives me says he does. "You need a drink, I think."

I don't have the chance to disagree before he's slinging an arm around me and guiding me out the door. "Where are we going?"

"Anywhere but here. I'm tired of this place, anyway," he announces. "Some situations call for a drink at a dive bar, don't you think?"

Truer words were never spoken.

CHAPTER 33

Dani

"They're both royally screwed up. They deserve each other," I say miserably, finishing my drink. Whiskey goes down way too smooth when it's mixed with ginger ale... and an aching heart.

"I think there's been some kind of a mistake," Mark muses, toying with his still half-full glass. Compared to the way he was slinging them back last night, he's exerting quite a bit of self-control. Or maybe he's hung over and taking it easy. Regardless, he seems to be thinking hard about what I just described.

"A mistake?" I snort, rolling my eyes. "I should've known better than to think I'd get any sympathy from you."

"What's that supposed to mean?"

"You're bros, right? You wouldn't take my side here. Not that I really have a side," I admit, staring at my empty glass.

"Thanks for giving me so much credit."

"Oh, come on. Don't you guys have a stupid code or something? Wouldn't he defend you if you were in his shoes."

"I never said I was defending him," he argues, leaning in. "I just said it seems like there's a mistake here, somewhere. I know Brock. And he wouldn't do this."

"Stop. Just stop, okay? This is the mistake, right here. Talking with you about this." I start to stand.

He holds me in place. Just as demanding as his buddy. "You're going to wait a minute, and I'm gonna clear up a few things for you."

I slam myself back onto the vinyl stool. He's right about this place being a dive. Windowless, a little grimy, and very depressing. Strangely, this is exactly what I expected when I came to Las Vegas. It was from a movie I saw when I was a kid. The sort of hole where losers come to drink their troubles away after taking a gamble and losing everything. I took a gamble, and look where it got me.

I sigh. "What could you possibly clear up?"

"For one thing, Brock is not in love with Charlotte."

I rear up instantly. "Bull. That's the reason he brought me here in the first place, because he's so hung-up on her." I pat his shoulder in a fake show of sympathy. "It's okay. I understand. Sometimes, even best friends don't share everything."

"You don't know half of what you think you know," he

insists. "Stop with the smartass comments and listen for a minute. Do you know how to listen? God, no wonder he likes you so much. You're both just as thick-headed as the other."

"Very nice," I mutter.

"I'm serious. Just listen. Please." He takes my hand, and holds it tight in both of his. "Brock isn't in love with Charlotte. He was never in love with her. I don't know what it was, really. Lust. She was his mistress, you know? He gave her lots and lots of money and she gave him sex. It's how he operates. I'm sort of the same way, so I get it."

Yeah, I know how he operates. He's giving me lots and lots of money too.

"When he found out she was getting married, he probably felt secretly relieved. Especially since, it's so obvious that it all was such a sham. I mean, me as the best man? When I never met the groom before this weekend, and was never friends with her? It's painfully obvious this was all an elaborate ploy to get under his skin, and looks like it failed big time too."

"Actually, judging by the fact that I found her in his bed, her plan worked very well."

"You still don't get it," he insists. "He didn't come here out of love for her, or some deep need to make sure she knows what she's missing out on by marrying somebody else."

"Oh, really? Because that's what he told me. He brought me here to make her jealous, because he couldn't stand seeing her marry somebody else. This was all a great, big lie. Like I said, I don't think you two are on the same page." I shrug, as though it doesn't matter, as though my heart isn't breaking into a thousand pieces. "I get it. You're guys. You don't want to talk about your feelings or whatever."

"You're the one who's two steps behind," he says. "Listen to me. Really think about this. Don't you remember Brock? From when you were kids?"

I stare at him. This is unexpected. For the second time today, I'm truly gobsmacked and have no idea what to say. "From when we were kids?" I eventually whisper, more to myself than to him. "I met him for the first time a few days ago."

He chuckles. "No. You didn't."

"What are you talking about?"

"Both of you know each other."

I frown. "We do?"

"Well, maybe you weren't good buddies or anything. But he remembered you the minute he saw you. He told me all about it. God, I wish he would've just told you. This would've all been a lot simpler."

"I don't understand."

"You went to the same school before you got sent away. Really think. Don't you remember him at all?"

He's right. I remember the feelings of déjà vu I keep getting every now and again. I think. I think hard, combing through memories I would've just as soon have forgotten forever. Brock, in my past. Was he there? In school? I hate thinking back to those days and all the boys who made fun of me and laughed, yet would stand in line to buy kisses—

And that's when it hits me. The dark-haired boy. Standing

against the wall, watching me. Staring. And how I cried because it was him I wanted to be kissing, not the poor fat boy in front of me. How ashamed I suddenly felt, knowing he was watching as I sold my kisses out of the sort of desperation only hunger can inspire.

"My God," I whisper, suddenly seeing everything in a different light.

"I guess you made a strong impression," Mark observes with a wry grin. "He's been crazy about you ever since those days, even though you disappeared. Maybe because you did, I don't know. He's never been able to get you out of his head. He always wondered what happened to you. When he saw you again, he had to find a way to keep you with him. So, he pretended to need you to show up Charlotte. That's all. It had nothing to do with her and everything to do with you."

I can hardly believe it. My heart's racing to the point where even breathing is a struggle. "Tell me—you're serious. Please."

"I'm serious. Which is why I'm sure what happened up there with Charlotte is a mistake. If I know her, she set it all up. Go to him. He's probably out of his mind by now, trying to figure out where you ran off to."

And I do, but only after I throw my arms around Mark's neck and squeeze as tight as I can. "Thank you."

"You want to thank me?" He laughs. "Defend me when he threatens to kick my ass for outing him like this."

CHAPTER 34

Dani

Brock is at the front desk when I race through the doors. I can hear his voice, raised over the general buzz of activity in the lobby.

"Nobody here saw where she went? You want me to believe you all happened to be looking the other way at the same moment in time? Is that the sort of fool you take me for?"

"Nobody takes you for a fool," the anxious concierge insists. He glances over Brock's shoulder and the sight of me makes his eyes light up in sheer relief. "Here she is, sir."

Brock spins, eyes wide.

I see him now. I really see him. He's more than just the dominating, self-assured control freak. He's out of his mind with worry about me. He thought I might have run off for good. He brought me here for himself. Granted, he could've just been honest with me that first night, back at his penthouse and saved himself a lot of money in the process.

"You're here." He looks me up and down, eyes darting back and forth as though he's checking for signs of damage.

It makes my heart go out to him in a way it never has before. "I'm here. And I think we need to talk."

"We definitely do." He leads me to the elevators. I catch sight of the concierge leaning against the counter with a sigh of relief. We don't say another word until we're back in the suite. The empty suite. Charlotte is long gone, thank goodness.

"You left before I had the chance to explain." He folds his arms.

Now, I notice for the first time how disheveled he looks. His polo isn't even tucked in. The collar is askew. I want to reach out and fix it for him, but I hold back. "I know, I should have waited and given you a chance to explain, but you have to look at it from my point-of-view. Would you wait around in the same room with that—that—person?" I gesture toward the bedroom and the empty bed.

He gets the hint. "You've got to know I had nothing to do with her being in my bed," he says, and sits on the sofa.

I do the same, leaving space between us. We're not out of the woods yet. I'm not ready to climb into his lap. "What happened?"

He runs a hand through his hair. "It's all so ridiculous and stupid. I feel so stupid. She showed up here with a bottle of red wine and put on this big show about being nervous for the ceremony, needing a drink with an old friend. Wanting to bury the hatchet. Wanting to start off with a clean slate, no bad blood between us. What a joke. But I let her in when she made a big deal about it. She poured an obnoxious glass for herself, but she did always like her wine, so I let it go. Until she spilled almost all of it on me." He grimaces.

"That's not even very original," I can't help but observe.

"No, it isn't. I got in the shower to clean up and when I came out...she was in my bed and you looked as if you had been struck by lightning. You have to believe me she was fully dressed when I left her."

I do believe him, but I can't make it so easy, either. "What happened after I left?"

"She tried to make it seem like she really just wanted me back, one last time with me before she got married, and you coming back was a surprise." His eyes glitter with fury. "I saw the text she sent you."

I had forgotten all about the text until that very second. Demanding that I come upstairs at once. I was so upset and so shocked I didn't see what was so obvious. Yes, she set us both up. Now that I have the benefit of a little time passing between my discovery and my conversation with Mark, I see just how absurd it all was. Like Brock would text me to come upstairs with Charlotte in his bed.

"I was very deeply hurt when I saw her there," I admit. "I know I have no right to be hurt, but that was how I felt."

"And I told her I'd never forgive her for what she did. I never forgave her for spiking your chocolates with strawberry juice to begin with, but this is inexcusable. I threw her out. I don't ever want to see or speak to that ignorant piece of trash again," he declares.

What a relief it is to hear that. "You never forgave her for that?"

"That was a low thing to do to you. You're just a sweet thing. You've never hurt her."

I tilt my head to the side as though I'm ignorant of the truth. "I thought you were still in love with her. I thought that was why we were here to begin with?"

For the first time in my presence, Brock flushes.

I actually got him to flush. It takes all my self-control not to jump up from the sofa and pump my fist in triumph.

"Yes. That. It's a long story."

"I have time," I assure him, leaning against the cushions. It's nice, feeling like I'm the one in control for once. Watching him squirm a little. Knowing who he really is, and how he knew me from the start goes a long way toward humanizing him.

"Suffice it to say I never cared about her. You're the one I wanted." He moves closer. Tentative at first, as though he fears I'll run away. When I don't, he gets more confident, and shifts closer. "I wanted you from the very beginning. I didn't know any other way to get you into my life."

"You could've just said you wanted to get to know me better," I suggest, raising an eyebrow.

"And if you said no, that would've been the end of it. I couldn't take that chance."

"So you chose to bribe me? Is that it? You took advantage when you knew I didn't have any money, and you're loaded?"

"I guessed you'd be too proud to accept charity, and that would be how you'd see it. As charity. I wanted to help you, and I still do. I want you to have every good thing you deserve. And you deserve a hell of a lot more than being so exhausted that you passed out on my bed. So, I came up with this plan."

"Scheme. Plot."

"Plan," he insists.

He's so close I can feel his breath on my face and smell his cologne as he wraps himself around my senses. He has a way of doing that. I could forgive him of anything in this moment. And there isn't anything to forgive, not really. I know why he did it. I wish he'd been honest, but at least I understand where he was coming from. And who wouldn't be flattered? Even touched?

I place my palm against his chest, and feel his heart pounding. He's so warm and real, and he's right here, wanting to be mine. I can feel it, and that knowledge crackles between us. It practically lights up the room. The energy between us is so strong I feel it on my skin. Even so, there's one thing he has to know first. I take a deep breath and say it, "I remember you now. From when we were kids."

A little of the light leaves his eyes. "What?"

"I remember you from that day. In the schoolyard."

"You do?"

He sounds so hopeful, like a little boy. It's enough to crack my heart open. I nod slowly. "You were standing there, against the wall. Watching me. I was so ashamed. Not just of what I was doing, but of me. For being poor, for having to sink so low as to sell kisses just to put food on the table that night. That was what made me run away, that shame."

"So it wasn't the fat, greasy, smelly kid who was waiting for a kiss? He's not the reason you ran?"

I frown. "No. I wished it was you I was kissing, instead of all the rest of them."

"That's good to hear. I always did wonder about that." He smiles, tilting his head to the side, staring deep into my eyes. "Because I wasn't the boy watching from against the wall. I was the fat kid who was waiting to kiss you."

The truth hits me like a slap in the face. That boy had dark hair too, and blue eyes. Only I hadn't been paying attention to him. I never had. I shake my head in wonder. "You were him."

He nods, and I see a sad flash of that bullied, unpopular fat boy all over again.

"I'm glad you are him. I never forgot you. I always felt bad about you. I took the money and never said thank you or gave you your kiss. You lost all that weight?"

He grins. "Yeah, I stopped eating peanut butter and jelly sandwiches and went to the gym."

"Oh Brock. I'm sorry if I hurt you all those years ago. I was just a child."

"I know. I never held it against you. And when you started to cry," he continues, stroking my cheek with the back of his fingers. "I wanted to make it all better for you. I wanted to protect you and comfort you. I loved you even then."

My eyes widen with surprise.

He nods. "Yes, I was a kid, but I did love you. I gave you all the money I had and told you to go home, because I didn't want to see you do what you were doing to yourself. It was tearing me up inside to see you cry."

I touch his face with a trembling hand. It was him. That sweet boy who shoved money into my hand and told me to go home. Who saved me from having to embarrass myself any further. Even then, all those years ago, he was trying to protect me. "Oh, Brock."

"I loved you then, and I'm in love with you now," he whispers, still holding onto my chin and using it to draw my face closer. "I love you, Dani."

"And I love you," I breathe the words out before a deep, searing kiss rocks me to my core and sets the rest of my life on course.

A life with this man, loving him and letting him love me. I couldn't ask for anything more.

EPILOGUE (1)

Dani
One Year Later

"To you." Brock raises the champagne flute with a smile, and touches it to the one I'm holding.

The fizzy liquid tickles my tongue. I take just the tiniest sip, savoring it right along with the feeling of success. "To me?" I point to myself. "You're the one who made it possible for me to go to school full-time, even over the summer. I never could've done it on my own. It would've taken two or three years at the rate I was going."

He looks so handsome, standing in front of the fireplace in the living room of our penthouse. *Our penthouse.* The thought of anything so extravagant being mine still surprises me, even after a year.

His smile widens. "I never really had the chance to do something truly worthwhile with my money. Charity, sure, but you gave me the chance to see the money being put to good use. I had a connection to the outcome. That meant everything."

"Well, gee. I'm glad I could do that for you." I giggle.

His lighthearted chuckle shows me how far he's come. Still serious when the situation calls for it, still a bulldog when it comes to getting his way—especially in business—but when it's just the two of us, he's like a totally different person. Relaxed, sweet, indulgent. Everything I ever could've asked for, but never thought existed.

The face of his Rolex catches my eye, and I let out a gasp of surprise. "We'll be late for our reservation if we don't get a move on. I know how much you hate being late."

"Who, me?"

I shake my head and roll my eyes. He hasn't changed all that much. Still a stickler for being on time. I had my choice of any restaurant in the city for our celebration dinner, and Lord knows there were plenty to choose from.

He's opened my eyes in a million ways, large and small, and our faces are familiar ones in at least a dozen or two of the city's top establishments. Even so, there's only one place that came to mind when it came time to choosing the location— the place where we had our first date, which wasn't a date at the time but was definitely the night when I first started falling in love with him. There's a beautiful symmetry to it.

It isn't until we've settled in at our favorite table that he leans over and takes my hand. "What's next, then?"

"Next?"

"For you? What do you want to do, now that school's over? Travel? Grad school? You realize you can do anything. I wouldn't deny you for the world. Just name it."

I pretend to think about it, looking up at the ceiling as I chew my bottom lip. "I don't know. There's a project I've had in mind."

"Really? You never mentioned anything about a project."

"Well, I only started really thinking about it a few hours ago."

"What's it all about?"

The best part of all of this is how innocent he is. Totally clueless. I don't know whether to laugh or kiss him. "It's sort of long-term," I start, winding my fingers around his. "Extremely, actually."

His eyes narrow. "You're considering something long-term and you didn't mention it to me until now?"

"I can't help it." I shrug, biting back a smile. "If anything, you're the one responsible."

"Me?"

I wait while the wheels turn in his head. Understanding begins to blossom. He glances at my still-full wine glass. Maybe he even remembers how I only took a slight sip of my celebratory champagne. I don't know what's going through his mind, exactly. Only that he's finally starting to get it.

"Are you—saying what I think you're s-saying?"

"I am," I whisper, suddenly nervous.

There is no smile on his face.

What if he's not happy? We've only ever spoken of a family in the vaguest of terms, agreeing that we'd want to start one sometime in the future but never stating when.

His face is still unreadable. A blank canvas. "You're going to have a baby?"

"Yes," I breathe the word out, and my heart is barely beating anymore. I want so much for him to be happy, as happy as I was when I first realized I was pregnant. I did three tests. I wanted to be absolutely sure. My head's been in a whirl all day, my imagination spinning all sorts of stories for my baby. Our baby. The person they'll become, thanks to us.

I only need to know that he wants this as much as I do.

He sits back in his chair and lets out a sharp burst of air. "A baby."

"That's what I said."

Just when I am about to die with unhappiness, his face just about cracks open, and my heart cracks open with it. Thank God.

His smile shines almost bright enough to blind me. "A baby? Our baby. Oh, Dani!"

"You're happy?"

"Happy? That doesn't even begin to describe how I feel right now. Did you ever have that feeling like all your dreams are coming true at once?"

I run my hand over the side of his handsome dear face and stare deep into his sweet blue eyes. There's nothing in the entire world that means more to me than he does. I've never felt as loved, supported, protected, and secure as I have in this last year of our lives together.

My eyes fill with tears of joy, and I nod. "Yes. I know exactly how that feels."

"Hey, you're not crying?" His voice is choked up. Brock simply can't bear to see me cry, even from happiness. It's such a funny thing because he is such a hard-headed businessman. I hear him sometimes talking on the phone in his study and his voice is so cold, demanding and foreign that I actually think it can't be him.

I'll go into the room out of sheer surprise and curiosity, and he will almost immediately put the person on hold and turn to me, his voice changed back to the one I am familiar with. No matter how long I am in that room, he will make whoever was on the phone wait. I've come to the conclusion that he is two different people. The one everyone else gets to see and the one he shows me. So, I don't do that to him anymore. Nowadays I wait until he comes out of his study, when he has removed and put away the mask he wears for the world.

I gaze at his handsome face now and smile. "I heard that a new baby is a very demanding thing and newbie parents get so tired they never have any energy for sex."

His head jerks back with surprise. "What?"

"It looks like we won't be having very much sex once the baby comes."

"We won't?" he repeats slowly, staring at me.

"Apparently not."

His eyes smolder with blue fire. "Not even if I do all the work."

"There is also the issue of lack of time."

He grins. "I'll be quick."

"So I was thinking…" I reach over with my index finger and very slowly start to push my clutch towards the edge of the table. His eyes flick over to my finger, then back to my face. As I continue to push my clutch, his eyes leave mine and follow the trajectory of the purse. As it reaches tipping point and falls, he returns his gaze to me.

"Oops," I say breathlessly. "I seem to have dropped my purse."

"It would seem that way," he says, his eyes unreadable.

"Would you be so kind as to pick it up for me?"

When he bends down to pick up my purse, I widen my thighs, and give him an eyeful. For a few seconds he seems frozen, then he jerks back up, his eyes blazing.

"Jesus, Dani, you've been walking around this whole time without your panties."

"Mmm…"

"Well, it's fucking time to get you home," he mutters.

I flutter my eyelashes. "Oh, but I've been waiting all night to have my dessert."

"You can have it to go."

I pout. "It's not the same. I want that cinnamon and pear thing they do with apple ice cream. The ice cream will melt by the time we get home."

"You're doing this deliberately, aren't you?"

"What do you think?"

"I think, Dani Saber, you should be very careful when you play with fire."

I laugh and lift my hand. A waiter instantly materializes beside us. "Can we have your pear tart to share please."

"Of course, madam," he says with a respectful nod before disappearing. I turn to look at Brock.

"You are in so much trouble," he warns.

"I know," I purr.

EPILOGUE (2)

(Brock)

I can't believe how damn long it took me to get her back home. But now that I've got her where I want her I'm going to teach her not to provoke me like that. Her smell never stops tantalizing me. A mixture of her apricot lotion, the almost child-like bubble gum waft of her shampoo, and the subtle scent of perfume on her skin.

I drag my thumb across her bottom lip. She gasps softly and closes her eyes. The sight of her like this, needing me so badly, still remains one of the sexiest things I've seen. A jolt runs up from my thighs to my balls, firing me up.

Hell, I'm so turned on my blood is pounding in my veins and I feel like a raging bull. She twisted my insides up so bad with her little restaurant stunt, I want to fucking tear her little two piece dress off and take her hard right here on the floor, but she's carrying my baby now. Our precious little child. And the need to be gentle overrides everything else.

She parts her lips and I push my thumb into her mouth. Catching my hand, she runs her tongue across the fleshy pad.

She bares her teeth, letting them catch on my skin, and I grin. Sometimes, I still can't believe this hot little vixen is *all* mine. That every fucking inch belongs to me. And only me.

I withdraw my thumb from her mouth, catch the back of her head, and draw her in for a kiss. A small moan escapes her lips as our mouths touch, and of course. The sound sends a bolt of desire right through my body. It's always like the first time with her.

I slide my other hand around her waist, pressing it against the small of her back, drawing her soft yielding body closer to me. The two of us have been built to fit together perfectly. I brush my fingers over the smooth strip of skin exposed by her velvet top riding up.

Our tongues meet. And…fire burns in my gut. I could kiss this woman for years. She is that addictive.

When I cannot bear the pressure inside my pants anymore, I move my mouth across her chin and down her neck, determined to taste as much of her as I can. After waiting for more than an hour while she purposely licked and sucked her spoon as if she was a porn star, I'm not going to wait another a second, or hold anything back.

I find that sensitive spot between her ear and her jaw, the one that makes her shudder when I press my lips to it, and let the hand on her back skim over her ass. She shifts her weight so she can grind up against me. Ah, my greedy, greedy little Dani. I look into her eyes and...such hunger. She wants it as badly as I do.

I lift her up and carry her to the bed. Laying her down gently, there is our baby to think of now, I climb on top of her. In the warm light of the lamp, her eyes almost glow with the intensity of her emotions. She stretches her hands above her head and, on pure instinct, I reach up and hold her wrists down, keeping them out of my way while my other hand roams across her body. Really, I want to punish her for making me suffer.

But there is the baby.

With my heart thundering in my chest, I sit up and, for a moment, indulge in my favorite thing, well, second favorite thing. Watching her. I look at her laid out under me. She looks so damn good. Actually, she looks incredible. Eyes half-shut, mouth open, her sexy little top pulled up to reveal her stomach.

Maybe I'll never see her like this ever again.

Soon her belly will become big and round with our child. Perhaps it will bring stretch marks. Things will change, move, shift. Her body will age, but I will always love her. She is my life. From the first moment, I laid eyes on her all those years ago my young boy's heart already knew it. All the other women in between...they were nothing. Not because of them, but because of her. I was always waiting for her to come back to me.

I reach down to kiss the spot an inch-and-half below her bellybutton and she moans softly. She is completely at my mercy. I can do anything I want with her. The idea never fails to tantalizes me. I lean down to gently nibble her earlobe.

"I'm pregnant, not suddenly made of glass, Brock. I *need* you to fuck me…like that night in Antigua." She murmurs the words directly into my ear, and I hear the craving in her voice. Deep in my soul something awakens, responds. She teased me in the restaurant because she wanted me to punish her.

She turns her head and without warning finds my mouth and bites down on my lip, hard. I welcome the pain, and taste her tongue, as our kiss becomes wild and raw. My need for her is deep, elemental.

My woman wants Antigua. Antigua, she will have.

I flip her over. She makes no sound as she buries her face in her folded arms. The sight of her absolute surrender is a thing of beauty. I let my eyes rove over her gorgeously soft skin and her curvy limbs, and her hair splayed out on the pillow while she waits to take every inch of me. It's almost enough to tip me over the edge. Lifting her by the hips, I slip a pillow under her. Then, I raise her sexy black skirt up to expose her glorious, glorious ass. Moving my palm over the smooth skin, I enjoy the shape and feel of the firm, warm flesh. When I pull apart her ass cheeks to inspect my property. She squirms. One day she will finally understand that I own all this. To check how wet she is, I insert a finger into her pussy. The girl is soaking wet.

She almost growls in protest when I pull my finger out.

I smile at the muffled protest, raise my hand, and let it crash down on her creamy flesh. The loud snap fills the room and is hard enough to make her gasp.

"Want me to stop?" I ask looking at the large red print of my hand on her skin

"No," she says from between gritted teeth.

My hand rises and falls all over those pale cheeks. Again and again, in quick succession, two, three, four, five, six, seven, eight, nine, ten...until her ass is shaking and glowing like a tropical sunset.

She whimpers and spreads her thighs, showing me the rear view of her pretty pussy. She knows how aroused I get when I see it from this angle. The lips pink and swollen with excitement. I stare down at her. Mesmerized.

The scent of her arousal is everywhere. The smell always brings out the animal in me. I move my face until it is an inch from her crimson ass so she can feel my hot breath tickling her pussy. She is so wild for it she wriggles and pushes her pussy against my face.

I begin to salivate.

Pressing the tip my tongue between her wet lips I lick all the way up to her clit. My plan is to tease her and just have one little lick, but her taste drives me crazy. Like a starved addict I start devouring her. Slipping my tongue inside her wet heat I lick every inch that I can reach. I palm her pussy and spread it open until she whines from the intensity of my lust. I circle, lick, suck, and bite that sweet clit until she howls with pleasure and release. I welcome her orgasm by lapping up all the sweetness that gushes out of her.

Watching her slumped, satiated and breathing hard under me, I quickly undress. Power surges through me, as I tell her to spread herself wide again. She immediately opens herself to me, and I shove my throbbing cock into her. She feels so tight and warm. She gasps and begs me not to pull out. I know she loves it when I am very deep inside her. In the beginning, she used to be so tight she couldn't take all of me, but slowly, I've trained her. Now I can bury myself to the hilt.

She slides her hands around my ass, drawing me closer.

"Play with yourself," I command. As soon as her hand disappears under her body to obey, I fuck her with all I have from behind. I see the cream from her pussy spread all along my shaft every time I slide out of her.

"Yes, that's it," she mewls, rolling her hips back and forth, to take me in deep.

When she pleads with me like this I'm barely able to contain myself. I grab her hips with both my hands as my thrusts become faster and faster, as she gets wetter and wetter. I can already feel my balls tingling as I get closer to coming.

I carry on slamming into her with such force and speed until there is no resistance. Our bodies are in perfect sync. The whole world outside our bedroom stops existing. There is no one in the universe but me and her.

"Don't stop," she begs. "I'm so close, don't stop."

Dani's moans get louder, and I feel her become tighter around me. Her pussy start pulsing and tightening with the onset of her climax. Suddenly she freezes. Her whole body becomes still except for her pussy which contracts wildly around my cock as if it is milking me for my seed. I close my eyes. I love that she has long orgasms. The way her muscles seize around me drives me crazy.

"Oh fuck," I grunt, when I can no longer hold back my own

release. I thrust my cock all the way inside of her and my cum shoots out of me. I stay deep in her pussy until I've filled her with my cum. Then I gently thrust in and out until I'm ready to slide out of her. Bending over I lick our juices from her pussy. She is still the best thing I've ever tasted.

Her eyes drift shut for a while. Sheis lost in the moment as I am, but she slowly opens them again and meets my gaze steadily. Her lips part, like she is about to speak, but nothing comes out of her mouth. Nothing needs to.

Silently, she gets to her knees. Cum leaks out of her as she bends her head between my thighs and takes my semi-hard cock inside her warm mouth. With absolute dedication she sucks it, moaning softly to herself with pleasure, until I'm hard again. Rising like a Goddess she shoves me down to the bed, and positioning her entrance over my hard cock, sits on me, burying my shaft all the way inside her sweet pussy. She rides me so hard with long purposeful strokes that her pussy sucks the cum right of out of me. Our climax is earth-shattering. Her mouth forms endless vows as I shoot my cream into her. When it is finally over, she lays her forehead against mine and stares into my eyes.

"I love you, Brock Garrett," she whispers.

I want to tell her how I feel, but I can't. I love her so much at that moment, words have become inadequate. I can only stare into her eyes wordlessly.

"You're supposed to say it back," she teases.

My answer is to kiss her eyelids, her cheeks, her lips, her throat. Tonight, I am too overwhelmed, but tomorrow I will do the thing I had planned to do at dinner time today. It was a good plan until she stole my thunder by telling me about our baby.

But tomorrow, I will take her to lunch and ask her to be my wife. She will make a beautiful bride. I can already see her, dressed in white walking up the aisle towards me.

My Dani. My world. My life.

THE END

SWEET REVENGE

RIVER LAURENT

BLURB

Great! My boyfriend of two years dumps me for another woman on the eve of New Year's Eve. Why? Because she weighs less than me. Thanks, James. Really. Thanks.
But, I'm not sitting at home crying for your sorry ass. I'm going to re-build the confidence you systematically destroyed.
And then I go out and the first person I meet is Ace. Whoa! It is sweet revenge all the way.

ISBN: 978-1-911608-13-4

❦ Created with Vellum

CHAPTER 1

DAWN

"Wait. What? Are you...dumping me?" I gasp in disbelief, as I lean back against the cupboard to steady myself.

"I guess so," he mutters, his shifty eyes sliding away.

"I guess so? What the hell does that mean? Are you, or aren't you?" I demand incredulously.

His sullen face swings back to me. His fists are clenched by his sides as though he's forcing himself to sit there and not bolt out of the front door. "All right, yes. Yes, I am."

"That's it? It's over between us," I say in wonder, just in case there is any doubt. It's always good to be completely clear about these things. When someone says all right yes. It's kind of a grudging agreement. It could mean no too.

He rolls his eyes. I hate when he does that. It makes him look like a dork. "That would be a safe assumption to make," he says, with a little snigger. He's loving this. This position of power. He told me that he's never been the one doing the dumping before. Every woman he's been with was smart enough to leave him first.

I shake my head as my brain tries to make sense of the thoughts flying through my head.

James and I have been together for two years. In fact, only two months ago he told me he was so grateful he had found me. We were perfectly matched and there would never be anyone else for him. However, our anniversary last week was kind of a mess. I somehow, convinced myself he was going to propose. Well, what would you think if you saw a bridal magazine stuffed under his pillow in his apartment?

When he didn't pop the question, and came up with the lame suggestion we get chicken take-out and just hang out at my apartment for the evening, I was pretty gutted. But I'm not one to give up at the drop of a hat and I decided to somehow salvage the night. I slipped into some expensive lingerie and swayed towards the bed in what he used to call my sexy walk, but he turned out the lights and fucked me for five minutes. It could have been longer, but it felt like less.

Not exactly the romantic night of my dreams. I had half a mind to flip on my vibrator and masturbate right there in front of him, but he started snoring next to me. Since I wasn't turned on anyway, there seemed to be no real point.

I stare at him now. "But it's New Year's Eve tomorrow."

He has the grace to look shamefaced.

"Why?" I whisper.

"Does it matter?" he snaps, flying upright and crossing his arms. Like a child who has been naughty and doesn't want to be told off. I'm so used to dealing with his tantrums and moods that I automatically reach out to comfort him, to make it all better even though he's a grown-ass man, and I'm the injured party here.

He evades my touch as if it is a branch of poison ivy and moves out of reach. My hand falls back heavily against my thigh. The slapping sound reverberates inside my skull. Wow! He can't even bear my touch. Okkkkkay. I take a deep breath and measure out my words slowly, clearly. "Yes, it does matter. I'd really like to know."

He snorts. "What difference does it make?"

I swallow the pure rage stuck in my throat. This asshole thinks he can walk in here and break up with me after he's wasted two whole years of my time, and not even give me a reason. I don't know what gave him that impression because I'm absolutely determined to find out why. Heck, I'll sit on his spineless back and squeeze it out of him if I have to. I straighten away from the cupboard. "Since it makes no difference to you, and as you don't have anything to lose," I point out through gritted teeth, "perhaps you will be kind enough to tell me what the *fuck* is going on here."

He turns back to me slowly, looking me dead in the eye, a nasty expression in his eyes.

Suddenly, I know what this is about. When he arrived early this evening, I think I already knew what was coming my way. Especially, when he sat on the edge of the couch without taking his shoes or coat off. He had no intention of hanging around too long. He wanted to get in and out. Some confident part of me wishes that I could back out of hearing him say it. I would love to airily walk him to the front door, while telling him to keep his pathetic reasons and fuck off out of my life, I'm just not interested to know.

But I can't do that.

I'm someone who needs to know. I need closure. If I don't get it out of him now I'll be calling him in a month or six months and asking him why then. So I'll be damned if I don't get him to spit it now. I square my shoulders. I'm a big girl. I can take it. Besides, I refuse to give him the satisfaction of thinking he crushed me like a bug under his shoe. After two years that's not how I'm going to let this end. Me splattered under his clumsy big left foot. Actually, for a man with such big feet he has a very small dick.

"You really want to know?" There's that ugly look again.

I nod.

He tosses his hands in the air in exasperation. "Just remember *you* wanted to go down this road."

"Just, spit it out, James," I growl.

"I met someone else, all right."

CHAPTER 2

DAWN

I was expecting it, but my stomach still drops. I look down at the ground in front of me. Yeah, I knew in my gut he'd been pulling away from me. I even briefly wondered if it had something to do with the new girl at his work he kept talking about. The girl with the lap-dancer name, but of course, I convinced myself that he was not that type of guy. He was faithful. He was in love with me.

"The slut at work?"

He flushes a deep red. "There is no need to get judgmental."

"Is it?" I demand, my anger boiling over.

"As a matter of fact, yes. Her name is Candy and she's not a slut. She's a great gal. She has a really lovely personality. She's always helping everyone."

My eyes widen. What is this fool doing now? He'll be telling me she's great in bed next.

"The first time we had sex," he confesses enthusiastically.

"She went down on me an...fuck, Dawn, she blew my mind. It was so much hotter than anything we ever had together."

I feel as though I am going to throw up. I press my lips together determined not to show myself up. Anyway, vomit is murder to get out of cream carpets. He notices the horror in my face and resolves to rub it in, for reasons that I can't quite figure out.

"I guess it's because she's hotter than you," he continues, getting into it now, apparently reveling in the power he has over me, the power to devastate me. "She's at least fifty pounds lighter than you..."

I can't help wincing as those words come out of his mouth. I can't believe he would say that to me. He knows how self-conscious I am about the way I look, and yet he can't resist twisting the knife deep into the most painful of my insecurities. This is starting to feel like revenge. He doesn't love me He hates me. An image of this woman pops into my head. She's slim and tiny and cute, and next to her I am a great heaving mound of flesh. And he *wants* to have sex with her... with the lights on. For more than five minutes.

I wonder how long he's been sitting on all of this, how many times he'd wanted nothing more than to tear me apart this way. I should just kick him out. And yet, I don't. Not yet, anyway.

"What about our tickets for tomorrow night?" They cost an arm and a leg.

"Uh, I thought since you probably won't want to go on your own anyway, I'll just take Candy."

I shake my head in wonder. What a bag of shit he turned out

to be. I paid for half of those tickets. My brain shifts gear. I never knew him. Now I need to know if I should get tested for anything. "How long has your affair been going on?"

"A month or so," he replies, and looks at me so brazenly, I wonder if he is even a little bit ashamed. Knowing he cares so little, that he's so happy to rub all this in my face, sends a flare of fury through my system. I'm not going to let him walk all over me like this. To be honest this man has been nothing but a burden for the last two years. I've done everything I could for him. I put his interest before mine, and now he's standing in front of me telling me he's betrayed me, and instead of being apologetic, he actually sounds victorious and proud of himself.

I know for damn sure that if he was cheating on me he wouldn't have used protection if he could avoid it. That's just the kind of guy he is. I guess I had always seen it, but now that it's laid out in front of me, so inescapably and utterly ugly, I have no choice but to accept that and try to protect myself as best I can.

"Did you use protection?"

He swallows hard. "No, but she's clean-"

"You're such a fucking piece of shit," I shout, rounding on him. Any sadness and hurt in my heart is replaced with burning fury. "Clean? How clean can she be if she didn't use a condom with you?"

"You're just jealous," he says smugly, and I think I see the hint of a smile on his face and it makes me so angry I actually want to scratch his lying eyes out.

"What is there to be jealous about?" I fire back, my voice

lifting in volume. I don't want this to become a yelling match, but if he's going to keep being such a prick…

He frowns, as though caught off guard, and I decide to go in for the kill just the same way he did for me when he told me how much slimmer this new girlfriend of his happens to be.

"You're a cheater," I begin, lifting my fingers and ticking off all his flaws one by one. "You're so cheap you used to make me cringe. You're rude to waiters. You snore worse than a pig. This new girl is welcome to you. Though maybe I should call her up first and let her know what she's getting herself into? Oh, and I nearly forgot. You're garbage in bed." There's a twist of triumph to my voice as I finish up all the ways that he's failed me over the last two years, all the ways he's been a shitty boyfriend to me.

His jaw drops.

I know I've hit a nerve, and it feels good for a moment, but I'm not a cruel person at heart and any kind of joy I might have gotten from seeing him so upset soon becomes a sour taste in my mouth and I find myself staring at him with more sadness than anything else. I should tear the shit out of him, and God knows that he deserves it, but for whatever reason it's just not fun right now.

I'm too hurt by his betrayal to really find any kind of consolation in the way he looks right now. I wish I could be a little more callous and cold and really go at him, chip away at his ego the way he's done with mine for more than a year now, but I can't. I'm just exhausted, and what I want more than anything in the world is for him to get the hell out of my apartment so I never have to see him again.

"If I was garbage in bed it was because I had a lump of whale meat in bed with me. Who can get turned on by that?" he yells.

"I hope I never see you again," I say slowly, and I really mean it too.

He opens his mouth to speak, but I've had enough. "You should leave," I point to the door, leaving no room for discussion.

"With pleasure," he sneers. Turning for the door, he walks out, and slams it so hard the walls rattle.

I close my eyes to quell the next wave of anger that overtakes me. I just want to run out there and scream at him for being such an asshole. The kind of idiot who seriously believes that slamming someone's door at this time of the night was a good way to make a statement.

What a fucking jerk.

CHAPTER 3

DAWN

I stand frozen, listening to his footsteps echo down the corridor. As soon as the entrance door of my apartment building closes, I find myself sinking into the couch. I stare blankly into space.

So this is what it feels like to be dumped. Well, I have been dumped before, but never by someone I've been with for so long, and not for another woman.

To my surprise there is more anger than heartbreak pulsing through my veins. Maybe the sadness will come later, but for now, all I can feel is a deep sense of betrayal. I trusted him. I thought we were both society's rejects who had found each other. Nobody wanted me and nobody wanted him and we had found a way to be good together. We once talked about making children. That was the first time I agreed to do it with him without a condom. I frown. Was he manipulating me even then? Because he never spoke about kids again after that.

God, how much time I've wasted on him.

My mind drifts back to when we first met. I was fresh out of college and had just started the internship that would one day become my full-time job. I was so confident, so passionate, so ambitious, and then I ran into this guy who had seemed so perfect for me. I was in advertising, he was in marketing. I actually saw us as a power couple. What a laugh. Thinking back now, I can see clearly that we were only a perfect couple for the first few months. After that all those subtle comments started. About my looks in general, my unfeminine laugh, but mostly my weight. All the little jokes. Once when we were going on vacation, he joked with the airline staff to seat someone equally heavy on the other side of the plane so that I didn't tilt the plane, and make it fly lopsided.

Slowly, with every strike he chiseled away at my confidence. Over time I no longer felt like a full-blown raging fire, I hated it, but I was slowly but surely being turned down to a fickle flame of my former self. I can still remember how it felt to be so full of light and energy, even if I can't muster up a drop of it for myself at this very moment.

I sit forward.

No, I'm not going to sit here feeling sorry for myself, and hope that somehow my life is going to get itself back on track. I'll do something about this. It's scary as hell, looking out on a life you never thought you'd face, but I can handle it. I can be single again. Maybe the lap dancer did me a favour when she went down on him.

I force myself to my feet and sway with the strong emotions running through my body.

Ignoring the voice in my head that seems intent on repeating the cruel words, specifically, about how much lighter his new girlfriend is than me, I begin to pace the floor of my apartment. I try to focus my mind on one thing at a time.

But those negative words nag at the back of my head. I have to address them.

What did I expect? I was making him feeling guilty and he needed an excuse. Attack is the best form of defense, and he knew exactly where to stick the knife to make sure that I'd bleed for hours afterwards. My weight is a sore point for me.

I've always been a buxom gal, but while I was with him I just couldn't stop the weight from piling on. To be fair it was partly his fault. I'd always stopped eating before seven, but he liked to eat late so he would often order fried chicken, or pizza late at night. He would have a couple of pieces, then he would force me to finish it, because he would make me feel as if wasting the food would somehow impact the starving children in Africa.

But now that I think about it. He was funny about my weight even when we first got together and I was still full of lovely curves, he never really paid me any compliments, or was positive about the way I looked. He preferred to make love with the lights off and it would often feel like he was trying to touch as little of my body as possible. The sex wasn't awful at the start, when the two of us were still getting to know each other, our likes and dislikes, but in the last six months it's been terrible.

I tried everything I could to switch things up, doing whatever I could in the vain hope that it might turn him on or get him to do more than roll on top of me, thrust for a few minutes, and then roll off. Oh, and of course he always loved his blowjobs. Those he had as regular as clockwork. Three sometimes four times a week. To the point, I felt that was all I was good for.

Filling my belly with his slightly bitter cum.

He would lay there with his eyes shut, groaning, "oh baby yes, yes, just like that," while I worked on him. I tried to pretend he was encouraging me, but I knew in my heart he was imagining some other woman. A woman he was actually attracted to. A thinner, sexier woman. One of those women I had caught him looking at. Women who weren't anything like me.

I guess even that should have been enough, over the last two years, to completely crush my self-esteem. I look down at my body now, in a pair of jeans and a sweatshirt, and run my hands over it. I don't like what I feel. The lumps and bumps. They were not there before I started eating his leftover pizzas and chicken.

I know I want to change, to forge a new life for myself. But his words are still ringing in my ears, along with every barbed comment he's made to me about the way I look. The comparisons to his friend's girlfriends, leaving pictures of slim, toned women on his computer, buying me clothes a few sizes too small for my birthday because he wanted to give me something to work towards.

But I can do this for myself.

That's what I have to keep reminding myself. If I want, I can lose this weight and get in shape. I know my thighs will never touch unless I starve myself, but I don't actually want that. I just want to be a size where I can be happy and feel beautiful.

I'll start again. I'll go out there and just be me for a while. Eat when I want to, have great sex with a man who actually thinks I'm attractive, and control my own television's remote. It'll be great not to be putting down the toilet seat every time I want to pee and cleaning urine off the floor every damn day. I won't have to hear his relentless disapproving voice every single time I do anything that he doesn't like, and quite frankly, that has become almost everything I do. God, the other day, he was complaining about the way I breathe. I can just do one load of washing a week instead of three. I won't have to suck his small cock again.

Yes, enough of being a doormat.

As I pace up and down the apartment, a smile forms on my face. I don't want to do this for revenge. I don't want to do this for him. No, in fact, if he had been a little kinder to me about all of this over the course of our relationship maybe I'd have been more inclined to do something about it before now. I stop pacing suddenly. I never thought about it before, but every time I so much as hinted that I was thinking about losing weight, he did everything in his power to covertly and subtly sabotage me. He brought sweets into the house, he ordered even more take-out at night and he made plans for us to go out for dinner when he knew I was planning on hitting the gym. Or he would suddenly want to cuddle on the couch with a movie.

So, I'm not going to do this to spite him. I'm going to do this in spite of him. Not because I want him back, or because I want him to regret his decision. No, I can't imagine any time soon where I'd want James back in my life. Candy is welcome to him. I just want to be happy with my body again, to prove to myself that the driven, passionate woman who had existed before James smothered her in fat is still buried inside me somewhere.

I'll start tonight. Right now.

CHAPTER 4

DAWN

I feel a wave of excitement overtake me. I don't have to worry about getting in the way of his schedule or go back and forth on what he might think of my evening's activities. I can just...do it. Whatever I want.

First things first. I march into my tiny kitchen and open the fridge. I take the tub of margarine from the shelf and, with great satisfaction, dump it into the trash can. I'm going back to butter. Next I open the freezer and trash the shitty soy milk ice-cream I had to pretend was a good alternative to real ice cream. Never again.

And tomorrow I will restock my entire kitchen. I'll get rid of all the bullshit low fat stuff packed with chemicals and go back to eating healthy natural food. Real food. I'm going back to my old ways. I'll eat only when I'm hungry.

I go back to the fridge and grab the expensive bottle of champagne I was saving for James's birthday by the neck. No need for that, anymore. I take it out, peel off the foil, and pop the cork. Champagne bubbles out and I laugh. I pull a flute glass from my cupboard and fill my glass. I wish I could share this bottle with Lisa, my best friend, but she's on holiday with her man. Never mind. This is about me taking back my life. Celebrating it.

I carry the bottle and the glass back to my living room. I sit on the couch and pull my legs up. I close my eyes and take a sip. Cold bubbles hit my tongue. Yes, this is the life. This is the way every break-up should be handled. I get up and put on some music. None of that pretentious rubbish that James makes us both listen to. No, just good ole, heartfelt music. I know exactly what I want to listen to as well.

Gloria Gaynor's powerful voice singing *I Will Survive* fills my living room.

I sing along as I drink my champagne.

"Go, walk out of the door," I yell as I dance around the room. If James were here now, he would be telling me that the neighbors downstairs will think a baby elephant has been let loose in my apartment.

But he's not here. So...yay! *I will survive.*

I drain my glass and refill it. By the time I've inhaled three glasses I'm decidedly merry. Candy is welcome to his sorry ass.

When Tom Petty and Stevie Nicks sing *Learning To Fly* a tear runs down my cheek. Not out of sadness, but just pure emotion. I just know that is going to be my song. I ain't got wings, but I'm going to fly. I wipe the tear away with the back of my hand.

And you know what else? I'm going to start my new life with a bang.

I look around the apartment for a hint of inspiration, and find it tucked behind the clock in my tiny kitchen. A pamphlet that was given to me when I signed up for the gym down the street from me. I had such high hopes about going three, maybe even four, times a week, but James took care of that enthusiasm. I pull the folded leaflet out, and my membership card drops out. I pick it up and look at it. It was more than a year ago. The thought makes me smile. He never truly could kill my spirit because I have been paying for it all this time. Just waiting for the right moment to reclaim my own strength.

That's what I'll do. I'll head down there right now and check the place out. I haven't been in since my induction, but I know the place is twenty-four hours, and that there are always members of staff on hand to help out.

I walk to my bedroom and go through my wardrobe to find something appropriate to train in. I pull out my sports bra and a pair of leggings, the thin fabric soft between my fingers, and I can't believe how nervous I suddenly am. It's just the gym, after all. But it's not just that. It's the enormity of changing myself, shedding off the last of the shit that James stuck me with.

I go back into the living room, down my last glass of champagne. I know I shouldn't be doing a work out after drinking, but the Dutch courage will be good to get myself through the door where I will no doubt be surrounded by perky, perfect gym bunnies. I wait for the alcohol to settle into my system and my head is buzzing slightly. Okay, I'm ready now. I can actually go out and do this. I want to do this. A good sweat is exactly what I need.

I don't have work tomorrow so I don't have to worry about

getting back at any time. I can stay out all night, if I want to, and who knows, maybe I will. Okay, that's wishful thinking, but nevertheless, it's nice to know I could if I wanted to.

I change into my gym clothes and neon bright shoes, then twist back and forth in front of the mirror, looking at myself, trying to find the confidence within me to step outside dressed like this. I don't look awful, well, I hope not, but the tight crop top displays all the lumps and bumps on my body that James hated so much. I must have internalized that dislike, because they are all I can see now, when I look at myself like this. I start to look for a baggy T-shirt to throw over my rolls of fat, but I stop myself. No. I go back to the mirror.

I press my lips together and roll my shoulders back and stare at myself.

"He's gone and you're not going to let him get to you anymore," I tell my reflection.

I grab a bag and a coat, and stride towards the door. I'm ready for this. New life here I come.

****

Sweet Revenge will be out late February.